THE ARTIST TYPE

BRIAN GLANVILLE

THE ARTIST
TYPE

COWARD-McCANN, INC.
NEW YORK

THE ARTIST TYPE

CHAPTER ONE

When I woke up there she was, lying beside me, and I thought, watching her, Jesus, if only she wouldn't talk. Because she always looked wonderful asleep, especially naked; there was nothing you could say against her body, and with her eyes shut and her mouth closed, her face was lovely, too. The sheet was pulled down so that one breast was bare; not big, I like them a bit bigger, but marvellously shaped, like an alabaster globe. I wanted to lean over and kiss it, but that would mean her waking up, and her opening her mouth and her eyes.

They were nice eyes, brown and big, I'd got nothing against them as eyes, only the expressions they had, or the expressions they didn't have. There was the Wounded Cow expression and the Poor Geoff expression and the *I* Understand expression, and they all made me say things I was sorry for. But her voice was worse, with its *wah-wah-wah*, a little-girl voice, a sloppy voice, making whatever she said sound silly, even when it wasn't. In fact there were times when I'd remember things she'd said, and they'd surprise me; I'd think, yes, that's pretty bright, that *couldn't* be her, till I realised it was the voice. She could recite the Sermon on the Mount in that voice, and it would sound like Little Bo Peep.

In the end I couldn't hold out; I ran my hand over her breast, my palm over the nipple, and up her nice long neck, and over her nice, high cheekbone, then I bent down and kissed her on the eye. A great shudder went through

7

her, like a ship suddenly going astern, and she smiled; it was a lovely smile, with her eyes closed, surprised and grateful, it made you feel, good God, did *I* do that? Then she reached out and squeezed my hand, really hard, as if she'd never let me go — which I knew was what she'd like — and I knew what the next thing would be, too, I was praying it wouldn't, but it was as sure as daybreak; she opened her eyes and asked, 'Geoff, do you love me?' And I bent and kissed her again, this time on the mouth, and said, 'Honey, you know I'm mad about you.'

She was really coming round, now; she got that Poor Geoff look in her eyes and said, 'You *know* she isn't any good for you.'

I said, 'Who?' stalling so I could get out of bed, and maybe out to the bathroom in time. She tried to pull me back and came half across the bed with me, then she let go and said, 'Audrey. She's destructive.'

We'd rehearsed this bit as well. I gave my sigh and said, 'Maybe you're right.' She said, 'You know I'm right. She makes you miserable.'

I beat her to the next line, 'And I make you happy.' I didn't say it, I was singing it inside my head, because I couldn't take it cold, not at this time of the morning. As I got to the bathroom I heard her say it, ' ... I make you happy,' and I turned the basin taps full on, to drown her out. I began to shave, and while I shaved, I started singing; that was another stratagem — you couldn't say much to a man who was singing, especially when he was shaving, too. I sang 'Some Enchanted Evening' in my Enzio Pinza voice, and from the bedroom she joined in; it shouldn't have annoyed me, but it did. It was something to do with her singing voice; not like her speaking voice at all, but what I called a Workers' Playtime voice — like those poor, playful old girls who warble away at lunchtime from some factory, all trills and terribly re*fee*ned, who haven't

8

been told that no one's been singing like that for years.

She came into the bathroom and stood beside me, singing, I saw us both in the mirror: me with soap all over my face, her like a choir girl, only a naked one. I thought, bloody hell, Webster Booth and Anne Ziegler, is this how they began the day? How could they stand it? She pressed her breasts against my back and put her arms round my waist; I stopped singing and said, 'You'll make me cut myself.' She said, 'You even look handsome with lather on your face.' I said, 'Lather on my face? That improves it.'

It looked the same old face to me, lather or not; too square and too much jaw, eyebrows too thick and mouth too wide, a face people would always say, well, *he's* all right, *he's* getting three square meals a day, however the hell you might be feeling inside, however much you might be going through.

I suddenly said, 'Jane, why do you waste your time on me?' and back it came, 'Because I love you.' I said, 'You waste that, too,' which hurt her, though I hadn't meant to; her face in the mirror started breaking up like a child's; I was afraid she was going to cry. She said, '*Why* wasted?' though God knows how many times she'd asked that, too, and I said, 'Look, I'm a swine, I've told you before,' and started washing the soap off my face. I said, 'You're too *nice* for me, I'm not *good* enough for you.' She said, 'You are, you are,' and put her head on my shoulder, and now she *was* crying, the tears were running down my shoulder, trickling over my chest. She said, 'It's John, you get together with him, you talk and talk and he poisons your mind against me. He's jealous, can't you see that?'

I said, 'John's got nothing to do with it, John's not interested in girls.' She said, 'That's just the point.' I said, 'It's me, not him. Not him, not you, not anybody.' Still, if she wanted to use John as her excuse it was better in a way, it was something she could live with; except it wasn't fair

9

to him, and it meant her always coming back for more. She said, 'You know what I think about him.' I said, 'Yes, yes, I know, I know, and it's rubbish,' and she said, 'You just can't see what's in front of your nose.' I thought, nor can you, dear, nor can you, and I slapped on shaving lotion, very expensive French stuff, with a lovely tingle, till she said, 'Do you like that, darling?' and I remembered that she'd bought it for me.

She'd bought so much for me, it was everywhere in the flat, I couldn't escape it; if I wasn't applying it I was wearing it and if I wasn't wearing it I was looking at it; lotions, hairbrushes, shirts, ties — dozens of ties — pullovers, fountain pens, blotting pads, china ornaments, I was surrounded by them. It was as if she said, look, they're all from me, I'm as good as here already; why don't I move in, too?

When I thought of that, I wanted to get out of the flat, get *her* out, I called to her, 'I must go soon, I've got this appointment, I'll drop you at your office,' and she said, 'You never *told* me.'

While I was dressing, she came in and dressed, too. She said, 'Shall I come round tonight? Shall I bring you something and cook it?' I said, 'I'm out tonight,' I was pulling a vest over my head. She said, 'Scampi,' as if she hadn't heard, 'you know you liked that last time.' These were the sort of conversations we had.

I put on my shirt; I said, 'A man from J. Walter Thompson, he's taking me to dinner,' and she came across with my cufflinks from my stud box and started fitting them in; she'd given me those, too. She said, 'Then come to coffee afterwards. To me.'

I said, 'I'll try,' and couldn't face her; the advantage of dressing, hurrying, was you didn't have to.

She went out to the kitchen, then, to make some breakfast; now and again she called to me from there, and I called back; vague sort of uh-huh, yes and no answers, as if I was still dressing. She always cooked me enormous breakfasts; this time there were sausages and fried eggs and a couple of rashers of bacon. I was getting fat again and I didn't want much, but eating was like dressing, you could hide behind it, and besides, if I didn't eat, it upset her.

She just had coffee and toast and sat there watching me, like a mother; I could feel her looking at me even with my eyes down, over the plate—she was enjoying every mouthful, more than I was.

I was just putting butter on the toast when she asked me, 'How's your play?' and I stopped with my knife in mid-air. She said, 'Did I burn it?' I said, 'No, it's just how I like it, perfect,' and she said, 'Have you finished the second act?'

I said, 'Not quite.' She said, 'I meant to ask last night. Can I read what you've done?' I said, 'It's a mess, you'd never understand it, all scribblings and crossings out.'

My play; she meant *her* play. She'd get that for me, too, if she could, if it was something that could be bought in a shop or cooked in an oven. 'I went to Harrods, darling, and I bought you your first night.'

She said, 'Will you tell me about it?' which gave me a way out. I said, 'Darling, you know how I hate talking about it while it's being written. Even to you.' Then I got up from the table and made a great production of hurrying. I got into my duffel coat, jammed on my deerstalker hat—she hadn't given me *that*—and hustled her through the front door.

The M.G. started at once, thank God, it had been trouble ever since I'd bought it three months ago; the ignition or some bloody thing; I reckoned that fifty thousand on the clock should have been a hundred thousand, at least. She said, 'Where's your appointment?' and I had to think. I said, 'Colman, Prentis and Varley, but I'll drive you down to Fleet Street.' We were turning into Cromwell Road.

11

She said, 'You needn't bother.' I said, 'Yes, yes, it's the least I can do,' then wondered what I meant and hoped she wouldn't ask me.

When we got to the Embankment, I was glad I'd come; no leaves on the trees, but the sun was shining and it had that *clean* look; the sky, the parapet, the water. I started to sing again, partly because I was happy, partly to stop conversation. I sang, 'You Are My Heart's Delight' in my Tauber voice, and she put her hands round my arm and squeezed it. It was pathetic, really, the way she'd take comfort from anything.

I dropped her outside her newspaper, she was the Foreign Editor's secretary; she said, 'Lunch?' not very hopefully. I said, 'Darling, you know I'd love to,' and she stood by the window, very wistful, holding my hand, saying, 'Ring me, won't you? Tonight? It doesn't matter if it's late,' and I half nodded and blew kisses at her, then drove off. I felt depressed, like I always did; guilty and irritated by her and sorry for her and resentful of her, all at the same time.

I turned back on to the Embankment and went straight home again. When I got there, I took out the play and looked at it; what there was of it. In fact I still hadn't written a line of Act Two, just a few notes scribbled in pencil that didn't add up to anything and probably never would. It was a comedy, meant to be, about a plumber in Battersea who starts painting pictures on the back of old biscuit cartons, and gets taken up by the critics and the dealers. I'd thought it was funny when I first dreamed it up, but somehow or other the steam had gone out of it, it didn't even make *me* laugh, now, so how could it amuse anybody else — except for Jane? In fact I'd have ditched it long ago if it hadn't been for her: 'Geoff, you *must* go on; Geoff, you really *have* got talent.'

Even now, holding it, reading it, my hands went tight

on the edges, I wanted to rip it across, then stopped at the very last moment; like I always did. I could hear what would happen. 'How's the play?' 'I've torn it up.' 'Oh, *Geoff*,' and tears, why did you do it? In a way, it would be tearing *her* up.

I was having lunch with Audrey; thinking of it made my stomach turn over. Would she be there, would she be late, how would she be when she got there?

It was all too damn much. I flung myself on to the sofa, put my feet up, shut my eyes and felt I never wanted to get up again. A terrible great sigh came out of me, like air out of a balloon. I thought, oh God, oh God, if I could only get free from them both; or, better still, amalgamate them. If Audrey was as sweet as Jane without being as soppy, or Jane was as intelligent as Audrey, but there you are, that's life; or my life, anyway. Jane was right; Audrey *did* depress me. But then Audrey was right about Jane, she indulged me, and that was sinister, too, in its own little way.

I lay there for about ten minutes, feeling like hell, then I got up and tried to do some work; some stinking little jingle about butterscotch. What the hell rhymed with butterscotch? Crotch? Hotchpotch? The worst of it was that, sitting there, I could see myself through both their eyes, Audrey sneering and Jane being sorry; such a *waste*, an artist like me. Sometimes I wondered whether I'd been right to freelance. At least when you were working in an agency you were all sitting there doing the same damned stupid sort of thing, bolstering one another, with telephones ringing, typewriters going, and a sort of pact never to say to one another, 'Christ, what a lot of balls' — so everything seemed real, at least until you got outside the door. But alone in your room, just you, a Biro and a block of paper, it all came home to you. You may never have been Olivier, you might not ever be a Bernard Shaw, even a Noël Coward, but you hadn't been put in the world to write hymns to washing powder and poetry to deodorants. But offices got me down, the theatre had spoiled me for offices. At the same time, I hadn't really got the freelance temperament, either, I need something to drive me; I'm always waiting for the phone to go or the doorbell to ring.

We'd had a promotion conference on this one. It hadn't been as silly as some of the others, with-it men in button-down collars and drainpipe suits talking dead seriously about what image to give a toilet roll, but it was bad enough. They'd had the account executive and the art director and the creative director and a couple of painters, a designer and a composer and me, and every now and then my eye would meet the composer's, and we'd both have to look away, to stop giggling. Still, you couldn't laugh at the money, and I'd promised to have it done for the end of the week.

It wasn't any good, though; I was blocked. I thought, Jesus, blocked on the play, blocked on a bloody advertising jingle. This was the sort of time I wished Jane was here, she'd say, 'Rubbish! They've got nothing to do with one another! The reason you can't write the jingle is you know it's beneath you.' But like this, on my own, I had a nasty idea it was all the same thing; I was just blocked: period.

I put a Dave Brubeck record on the record player; it cheered me up, but it didn't unblock me. Then I rang Ted Warren, the composer, and asked him if *he* had any ideas, I said, 'If you've got a tune, maybe I can find some words for it.' He said, 'If you've got some words, maybe I can find a tune,' which was the way we usually did it, and had agreed to do it, this time. I said, 'Maybe if I came over, and we worked on it together … ' but he had a recording session, or he said he did; he had dozens of irons in the fire and he'd never give you a minute more than he had to: I couldn't blame him.

So I sat down to it again, there was no alternative, and got nowhere, until John rang up, and we chatted about the children's book we were trying to do together, and when I'd eventually hung up and poured myself a whisky and played myself another record, it was time to go out to lunch.

We were meeting at the Trattoria Firenze, in Greek Street, it was a place I liked but couldn't really afford; you could never get out below three or four quid for two, but it was her favourite place, and that was that. I was short again today, and I hoped they'd take a cheque. Sometimes when I was with her I'd think, Christ, you might offer to share, but she was the sort of girl it would never occur to, even now, with her Jag and her flat in Sloane Street, whereas Jane would pay for both of us if I let her, and sometimes I did.

She wasn't there when I arrived, I didn't expect her to be. I went down below, where we always went, to a table in the corner, and ordered myself another whisky. The waiters were all Italian and wandered around in rather poncey blue monkey jackets, and there were trellises and grottos and lighted panoramas all over the place. After twenty minutes I wondered if she was coming—twenty was par for the course, half-an-hour meant she wouldn't turn up—but she came after twenty-eight; she never apologised.

As usual she looked so good I just felt grateful she was there. She had a marvellous eye for colour, people were always turning to look at her, and they did now, as she came round the corner of the stairs. She was wearing red; a red coat, a red suit, very narrow, and on the back of her head, a little, red straw hat. I got up and kissed her and said, 'You're beautiful,' and she smiled and said, 'Do you think so?' I said, 'I always think so,' and we sat down. She said, 'Then it's not so much of a compliment, is it?'

I said, 'You look beautiful in different ways, that's all.

Today you look like ... I don't know. A beautiful redcoat.'

She said, 'I'll carry my umbrella over my shoulder, shall I?'

The head waiter came over and made a great production out of welcoming her: 'At last we see you again, Signora ... ' then they brought us the menus, and while she read it, I was looking at her.

She'd got a cold face, really; I knew that, but it didn't make any difference, any more than it made any difference that she was delicate and slim. In fact the funny thing was that I was her physical type, and she wasn't mine. I'd said to her once, in bed with her, 'What do you *see* in me?' I'd really meant it, and she'd said, 'Your body, of course — when there's not too much of it.' I said, 'You make me sound like a stallion,' and she'd said, 'Well stallions are fine; as long as they're just being stallions.' She always knew where to jab.

Her eyes were a very pale grey, long and narrow, Chinese eyes, almost, except for their colour, and they gave the tone to her face; cool, not in the jazz sense — though she was that, as well. Her nose was long and straight, just slightly turned up at the bottom, her mouth was rather full, and she was blonde. I loved the colour of her hair, there was something metallic about it. Sometimes she messed around with it, she had it dyed fairer or darker, and I'd plead with her to let it grow back again. She was always being painted, she knew dozens of artists; I think it was this Mona Lisa thing about her, as much as anything, this enigma. Even when she laughed, she seemed to be keeping something back, she was like a spirit of some kind; a nymph or a mermaid.

She said, 'And what have you been doing?' in a bantering voice. Sometimes I thought she was ashamed of herself for fancying me, and that this was at the bottom of the digs and all the little cruelties.

16

I said, 'Oh, the usual crap. You know: jingles.'

She said, 'Jingles!' and her face lit up. She was on the scent. She asked, 'About what?' and I looked away from her and said, 'Butterscotch.'

She laughed, like I knew she would; she laughed a surprising amount, though it was the sort of laugh you might have expected from her, full throttle but not happy.

I tried to come in on it, I said, 'Anyway, it's better than deodorants.'

She said, 'Why don't you appear in commercials again, then you could sing your own jingles? You'd probably be unique!' I said, 'Damn funny,' and picked away at the menu card. She had this effect on me, making me sullen, and I couldn't help it, though I knew it amused her. I said, 'You find me something better to do, and I'll do it.' She said, 'Go back on the stage,' and I said, 'We've been through that.' She said, 'It's what you do best.' I said, 'It's what I *did* best. Come on, let's order.'

She said, 'Do you remember *Hay Fever*, at Littlehampton?' I said, 'Yes,' and we hammed a few lines. That was where I'd met her. She'd just left the Central School and I was the bright boy from RADA with the gold medal. She'd never been very good, she couldn't lose herself in anything, that coldness got in the way, or maybe it was fear; fear of *being* lost, I was never sure. But she'd always looked so good; I think she would have been better in the cinema, and that was where she might have ended if this poor, rich sod hadn't come along and married her.

We were both of us laughing by now, and she'd given up baiting me. We were always safest talking about Littlehampton; the digs we'd stayed at, the others in the rep., and the way the director tried to fiddle everybody out of what he owed them. They were good days, I suppose, and they looked better from a distance; when you're

17

as young as that, you think you can move mountains.

She asked me suddenly, 'How old are you now, Geoff?' and I said, 'Thirty,' and she whistled. I said, 'Tell me I look younger.' She said, 'I'm so used to you. You always look the same, to me. One loses track, though, doesn't one?'

I said, 'I wish one did.'

Because thirty was hell, thirty was the moment of truth, the bloody watershed. From thirty, you looked back at all the things you hadn't done and looked ahead to all the things you knew you'd never do.

She said, 'Cheer up, you'll probably be at your best at forty. Lots of actors are. Then you can go back and play heavies, instead of juveniles.'

I didn't smile. I knew I'd never go back, and she knew it, too. It was those six months that did it, after Windsor; six months of bloody Labour Exchanges and landlords and working in the post office and washing people's floors and eating in Lyons, if you were lucky. Six months of wondering whether you were really any good, and if you'd ever work again, till when the work came at last, it had gone, you were hollow inside, the lines made no sense and the stage was something you had to force yourself on to, like walking through fire.

So then there was the male modelling and the telly commercials, and after being in them and hating that, the next logical thing: writing for them.

I said, 'What are *you* doing?'

She said, 'Going to Paris'—she was always going somewhere—'to see the Delacroix exhibition. Come with me,' and I said, 'How?'

She said, 'What about all the money you make from your commercials; that's surely the only reason for doing them.' I said, 'I wish it was.' She said, 'Then why don't you give them up?' I said, 'Here we go again. For what?

She said, 'For anything.' I said, 'I'm writing a children's book.' She said, 'I know. You told me months ago. You're doing it with that friend of yours. Well, there you are. If that comes off, you can be another Enid Blyton; she's rolling in money.'

I said, 'God, you're in a bitchy mood today.'

She said, 'Nonsense, I'm trying to be helpful. You always want women to mother you.'

I said, 'You'd never do that.' She laughed and said, 'No, I wouldn't.'

I don't think I've ever known a woman less maternal. She knew it herself, and she could reel you off a catalogue of reasons; transferences and traumas and father fixations; I suppose they helped her to live with it. Sometimes she'd start psycho-analysing me; I was insecure and dependent and I was mother-identified or auntie-identified, or whatever the hell it was. I'd tell her, 'Yes, yes, yes, it's all probably true, if I could understand it, but what bloody use is it to me? Does knowing about things change *you*? All it means is that when you do something nutty, you can tell yourself afterwards why.' She said, 'Which helps you not to do it again.' I said, 'If you're lucky,' and she said, 'I know perfectly well I'm self-destructive.' I said, 'There you are; you know. So what?'

But at the moment she was laughing at herself as well as me; this was something we shared, this knowing she could never be maternal. She said, 'Still, if you can write children's books without being a father, an *acknowledged* father ... ' I said, 'All right, all right.' That was another place that hurt. She said, 'I simply meant there might still be hope for both of us.' I said, 'You mean you'd like to be a mother, one day?' She said, 'No, of course not.' Which, funnily enough, was about the only thing she had in common with Jane. Jane didn't want to be a mother either.

A French film director came across from another table and kissed her hand; her eyes shone, she loved that sort of thing. She introduced us and he just about acknowledged me, what stone did you crawl from under? I often got that from her famous friends. When he'd gone, she said, 'Louis's brilliant. Did you see *Pends-toi, Pauline*?'

I said, 'No, but I can imagine it. Full of shots between the cameraman's legs, and it all takes place on a railway station.'

She said, 'You're jealous!' I said, 'Am I? I got the impression *he* was jealous,' then the waiter brought our coffee. I said, just idly, 'What are you doing this afternoon?' She said, 'Nothing much. You can come to tea, if you like,' and this shock went through me, through my stomach, my chest, my solar plexus. I said, 'Yes, okay.' I could hardly get it out, and it frightened me, this power she had over me, this hold I couldn't break.

We drove separately down to Sloane Street, she in her Jag, me in my old M.G. I let her go first, mostly because I never liked driving in front of her. She was a bad driver, impatient and fast; she jumped lights, cut in on people, took silly risks; in a way, she drove like a man, more than a bad *woman* driver. She was always getting her licence endorsed.

It was weeks since I'd been in her flat. It was like her, very elegant and expensive, nothing vulgar, paintings covering the walls, none of them earlier than Cézanne, eighteenth-century Italian furniture, very nice to look at, very hard and uncomfortable to sit on, welded sculptures writhing all over the place. I sometimes thought it was too good to live in. In a way, it humiliated me, I always wanted to get out of the drawing-room as quick as possible and into the bedroom, where at least I had some sort of equality.

When I'd helped her out of her coat I put my arms

round her and tried to kiss her, but she wriggled away with that teasing smile and said, 'I said, tea,' and when she'd made the tea, in a Georgian silver teapot, she sat on a chair behind the little table and I had to sit across from her, on a bloody hard sofa. She pointed things out to me that she'd bought since I'd been there—a sketch by Giacometti, a new mobile—and I wondered how long she was going to keep it up. We always had the preliminaries, it was no use trying to rush them; though sometimes they weren't preliminary to anything.

So we drank tea and I kept looking at her, her face, her hair, her beautiful, long legs, the triangle of bare skin left by her jacket, and she smiled, to watch me watching her. She said, 'You're not talking. You came to amuse me.'

I said, 'Give me a minute: I'll stand on my head.' She said, 'Could you?' I said, 'Yes,' and got up and did it, with the money falling out of my pockets. She said, 'Very good. What else can you do?' I said, 'Oh, plenty of things. Catch biscuits in my mouth,' and I knelt up with my hands dangling in front of me, like a performing seal.

She said, 'Let's see you,' and threw a biscuit at me; I snapped at it, but it hit me on the chin and bounced off. She threw another one, then another, laughing more and more; on about the sixth or seventh, I got it, and she applauded. I ate it, no hands, biting it in half, tilting my head back, catching the other half before it fell, then swallowing that, then I went, 'Honk-honk-honk!' and came shuffling across the floor towards her; by now she was practically helpless.

When I reached her chair, I went on honking, flapping my fins and nuzzling into her lap, till she fell forward with her arms round my head and I toppled backwards so she came with me, and there we both were on the floor, she laughing, me still honking.

This was the moment, I knew. I pulled her face towards

mine and kissed her. Her tongue came into my mouth like a piston; it was always the same with her, everything or nothing. I slid my hand up her thigh, gently, over the muscle, and she grabbed my cock, hard. She said, 'Come on, come on!' then we were up from the floor, still locked together, moving towards the bedroom.

I'd never known a woman make love like her; convulsively, as if she was possessed, given up completely; not to you, that was what hurt, but to *it*, to making love, to sex. She bit and she scratched and she moaned and she twisted in a way that made you feel, I'm being used; it needn't be *me*. And besides, there was always this pain—was it the last time, would it ever happen again?—so that I'd touch her and kiss her and feel her, almost to commit her to memory, so at least I'd have this image I could carry around with me.

She must have come two or three times, and at the end she gave me this tremendous squeeze, her arms round my waist, her legs round my legs, then wrenched away, lying on her stomach, her eyes closed, her face turned towards the wall. I touched her shoulder, but she twitched, like a horse with a fly, and I took my hand away. The hating time came now. I wished it was later, so she'd fall asleep; or I could.

I got up, and went to the bathroom. When I got back, she was lying just as I'd left her; her eyes were open, but blank. I'd like to have got back into bed with her, at least to have gone up to her and kissed her, but I knew what would happen if I did. So I dressed very slowly—she still didn't move—and when I was dressed, took out my cigarettes and lit one. I had a gold case; the lid sprung up, and inside was engraved, 'To Darling Geoff, with love from Jane.'

I asked her, 'Cigarette?' and she said, 'Yes,' just like that, very short and cold. I went round her side of the bed, like a nurse to a patient; she raised her head off the pillow so I could put a cigarette in her mouth and light it, then let it fall again. Her expression didn't change.

I sat down in front of her dressing-table and started fiddling with the bottles of scent; in the mirror, I could just see the top of her head, and smoke curling up in grey spirals. I said, 'I'll go, if you like.' She said, 'Please yourself,' and I shut up. The one thing I really wanted to say was, 'I love you,' and I'd tried that before: 'Do you?'

I don't know how long I sat there, she lay there, neither of us saying a word, half-an-hour, perhaps, but you can't measure that sort of time. While it lasts, it lasts for ever.

It got dark, the shadows crept across the floor, until we were in twilight. She asked me for another cigarette, and we went through the same performance; now, as she smoked, I could see the tip glowing in the dark. She said, 'Why don't you go and get yourself a drink, and get me one?' and I went into the drawing-room and poured two whiskies; mine must have been a quadruple.

She said, 'Someone's calling for me at seven.' I looked at my watch and said, 'It's half past six, now.' I went to the bed again, bent over her and kissed her; not on the mouth, the cheek. I said, 'I'll phone you, honey,' and she said, 'Yes, phone me.'

Down below, I sat in my car, shaking. I started the engine, then turned it off again; I wasn't fit to drive. I thought, that's it, fuck her, that's the last bloody time, yet the terrible thing was I knew it wasn't. Tomorrow it would still hurt, but I wouldn't be sure, and in a week I'd be ringing her again.

I looked out of the window. I was parked by the railings of one of those gardens where nannies take children, and the gate's locked, to keep out proles like me. About fifty yards down stood three phone boxes. Almost without thinking I got out of the car, went into one of them, and dialled Jane's number. Of course it had to be Marion, her bloody cousin, who answered.

I said, 'Hallo, it's Geoff. Is Jane there?' and you could hear the icicles forming. She said, 'No, she isn't' — she was obviously delighted. I said, 'When will she be back?' She said, 'I've no idea.' I said, 'I see, *thank* you,' and hung up. There was no use leaving a message, ten to one she wouldn't give it to her, and if she did, I'd no idea where I'd be. I couldn't go home, I had to see somebody.

I drove down the Kings Road to the Markham, but it wasn't the same nowadays, there was no one there I knew, so I got in the car and drove to Holland Park, to John's.

He was in, thank God. He opened the door, took one look at me, and said, 'Jane or Audrey?'

I said, 'Audrey,' and came lurching in, into the sitting-room, neat and tidy like it always was, on to a sofa, putting up my feet; which I knew he hated. The record player was playing Eartha Kitt — he loved her, I thought she'd had it years ago. There were creature comforts every-where, cushions and rugs and hassocks, John's own paint-ings on the wall — two landscapes, a portrait of me that embarrassed me, it was so bloody *jeune premier* — and dozens of those tall art books in the bookshelves.

He said, 'It's usually whisky for Audrey, isn't it?' and poured me one, a sherry for himself. He was tall and thin, he had red hair that was going — which upset him — and he had this *discreet* way about him, just this side of camp, very quiet but somehow sheathed. We'd talk about my sex life, never his; I was never quite sure which he liked best, the stories about my making out or the stories about my getting hell. I took it for granted he was queer, but it was something we neither of us mentioned. Sometimes I thought it was a bit unfair, my telling him my troubles and never hearing his, but this was how he wanted it.

He was glad tonight, it was obvious; glad I was con-

24

fiding in him, and glad there was something like this to be confided. He said, 'And do you really love her? After that?' I said, 'Yes, worse luck. That's the whole bloody trouble.'

He said, 'You really ought to *know* by now.'

I said, 'For God's sake, I told you, I'm in love with her, fuck her. That's what it's all about, you know that.'

He said, 'Yes, and so does *she*.'

I said, 'This was the worst yet.' I put my head in my hands; the pain was still too much.

He said, 'Remember she's probably just as unhappy as you are.'

I said, 'Are you kidding? She uses me and when she's used me, she throws me out. That's all there is to it.'

He said, '*Happy* people don't do that.' I said, 'All right, then, she's unhappy. What good does that do me?' and I got up and began walking about the room. I knew he didn't like that, either, but I couldn't help it; if I sat still I felt trapped and suffocated; moving eased the pain. I said, 'You know something else? The most disgusting thing of all?' He said, 'What?' pointing like a dog, and I wondered should I tell him, then did. I said, 'When I came out of the flat, who do you think I tried to ring? Jane!' He said, 'What would you have told her?'

There was this undertone, this almost gloating interest, and I knew I'd been wrong, I shouldn't have told him. I said, 'Nothing. What *could* I have told her?' He said, 'Everything. She'd probably have been glad.' I thought, like you are, and he said, 'She'd have told you, there you are, you see, you should stick to me,' and I realised he was probably right.

He said, 'Cut off in stages; you'll be amazed how well it works. You say to yourself, I'll keep away for a week. Then you extend it to a fortnight, then a month, and before you know where you are, three months have passed

25

and the feeling's gone. You're free.' I said, 'I've tried that,' and I had. In fact it was always happening to me, whether I liked it or not, because she was for ever going off some-where: America, the Caribbean, the South of France. When she went it would sicken me, it felt like an amputa-tion, but I'd always tell myself the same thing: make the best of it, take advantage of it, get used to being without her — but it never worked.

Sometimes she'd send me a postcard or two, with a couple of words on it — one of those blue skies and sunshine cards — and that would keep it alive. Or she wouldn't write at all, and *that* would upset me. One way or another, she'd be in my mind. I'd wonder what she was doing at such and such a moment; or who she was with. I'd picture her stretched on the beach in a bikini, she loved the sun, or draped on the deck of someone's yacht, or swimming, or dancing, and I'd ache. Because in all these pictures I imagined she'd be happy, smiling or laughing, and I knew for a certainty I never came into her head. When she got back, there I'd be, good old Geoff, always available, the stallion; not too bright, not successful, but there for service, when she wanted it. I'd wonder how many other stallions she had in London, or where she found them when she went away; beach boys, maybe, lifeguards, and all those gigolos in the international set.

Then, just as I was coming to terms with it, when I'd got myself involved with some bird or other, she'd be due to come back. I'd always know the date, of course, how-ever hard I tried to forget it, and the nearer it got, the more I seemed to be hypnotised by it. I'd tell myself, screw her, I'm finished with her, it's over and done with. Then, with a couple of days to go, I'd start thinking, I'm damned if I'll phone her this time, she can phone me. But after a week or so — ten days was the longest I'd ever managed — I'd be on to her. She never got through to me.

I said to John, 'Let's work on the book.' I didn't want to, but it changed the subject; so he got out the drawings he'd been making. He was very neat and clever; decorative, really, almost fussy; the detail was always the best thing about it. I suppose *it* was camp as well; I'd shown a few drawings to Audrey once, and she'd laughed, she'd said, 'Aubrey Beardsley! Aubrey Beardsley, out of Mabel Lucie Attwell!' but it was still good in its way.

I envied his application, he was like a machine, turning it on or off whenever he wanted, and I knew I drove him mad at times, sitting around, drinking, chatting, playing records, when he wanted to get down to work. He taught a little in an art school, did book jackets, some commercial work—which was how we'd run into each other—and he'd hung a few pictures in the Royal Academy, though the dealers wouldn't look at him. This didn't surprise me; painting like his wasn't in just now and perhaps it never would be; on the other hand, he'd always make a living.

An agent was handling our book; he'd already got us a hundred and fifty quid advance from a publisher; the only thing that was really holding us back was me. The story was called *The Inquisitive Camel*; a camel who sets out across the desert to try and solve the riddle of the Sphinx. It was all very simple, and I kept the text as concise as possible, just a few lines on every page, beneath a big, coloured picture.

John said, 'Any ideas?' and gave me this ironic smile of his, which seemed to put *him* down at the same time as it did you. I tried to think, I was still suffocating in this great fog of misery. He looked at me like a school teacher and said, 'The monkeys at the oasis.' I said, 'Oh, yes, that's right,' and he smiled at me again and said, 'You haven't given it a thought, have you?' I said, 'Yes, I have,' and screwed my eyes up, trying to remember if I had or not.

John said, 'What *kind* of monkeys?' I said, 'Baboons, definitely,' God alone knows why, and he said, '*I* thought more like these,' and showed me a sketch he'd done, in which the monkeys looked like marmosets. He said, 'I thought they could be organ grinders' monkeys, lost ones; rather like *Peter Pan.*' I said, 'What a good idea,' and he beamed at that, he said, 'I hoped you'd think so.'

The phone went then, and he had one of his guarded, *sotto voce* conversations, full of hints, very short; you almost expected him to cup his hand over the mouthpiece: 'Yes ... very well ... *there*, then.' They were boy-friends, obviously, but you might have thought they were spies from the way he went on. I didn't care one way or the other, but I knew it embarrassed him for me to see this side of his life. When he put down the phone, he spoke right away, like he always did: 'I think they ought to have tails' — as if to cut it off, as if it hadn't happened.

I said, 'Yes, I suppose they should.' I still wasn't plugged in. I made a great effort, I tried to clear my mind and think about camels and monkeys and palm trees and Arabs, but it still kept wandering back, it was too big a step; out of this fog, into a children's world, where everything's ridiculous until you accept the logic of it. And John began to get tetchy, saying, 'Look, if you don't *want* to discuss it now ... ' and, 'You *can't* drag Touaregs in again, we had *them* in the raid on the caravan.'

I knew how he felt. Here we were, he and I, all cosily installed up here, ready to work together, and all I could think about was some damn woman who didn't even want me. By the time I realised it was hopeless and said I thought I ought to go, he was really sulking; sitting there with a painting on his lap and his head bent, almost like a spoiled child. He said, 'Well, there's not much point in staying, I suppose.'

I said, 'Look, it's my fault. I know I shouldn't have come.'

He managed to say, 'All right,' and nod, but you could see how it was choking him.

I let myself out, and I drove home. When I got there, I took a sleeping pill; I knew what kind of night I was in for if I didn't, and I still had a bad hour or so. The thoughts spun round and round in my head in horrible concentric circles leading back and back and back to the middle, and in the middle was nothing; a hollow. Nothing now, nothing in the past, nothing for me in the future. At the same time, that nothing was the kid, the face in the cradle looking at me; he was the symbol of it, he always would be, as long as I knew he was alive. My son. My nothing-ness.

I'd said get rid of it, but she wouldn't, and I knew why she wouldn't; because if she kept the kid, she thought she might keep me. We'd split up when she was four months gone; she'd said, 'I'll have it, and I'll keep it.' That was blackmail, too; as long as she kept it, I might come back to her.

When it was born she sent a message to me, and like a bloody fool, I went, I weakened. She was in this Stone Age place near Waterloo, in a room with about six others, with the kid in a cradle by her side; when I came in, she was crying and it was crying, and it hit me at once, the moment I looked at it, all squashed and ugly and pathetic, with enormous eyes. I wanted to cry, myself.

I'd brought her daffodils, and a box of chocolates. I put them on the bed, and she put her hand over my hand and smiled at me, and I thought what a bastard I am, what a bastard, which I suppose was what I was meant to think. I stayed for ten or fifteen minutes, not speaking much, just holding her hand, looking at her, looking at the baby, and thinking that I ought to marry her. I knew the other women there were goggling at us, it was a great treat for them, but it didn't worry me, they could go to hell.

She'd said, 'You'll come again, won't you?' and I'd said, 'Of course I will, I'll come tomorrow,' I really meant it, and that night I got a plane to Mallorca, and stayed there all the summer. When I got back, I heard she'd had it adopted.

I'd only bumped into her once, since then; one Saturday morning, walking along the Kings Road. She was in a headscarf looking very pretty; very bright and brittle. She'd said, 'Hallo, how are you?' in a cocktail-party voice, but I couldn't play it like that. I'd said, 'Let's have a coffee,' but she said, 'I've got to rush, I haven't got time,' and I'd stood there, willing her to stay. I'd said, 'Where is he?' She'd said, 'Who?' then her smile had gone, melted, just like that, she'd said, 'An architect's family. He's very happy. I never see him,' then the smile came back again, she said, 'Goodbye, Geoff!' and went off very quickly, trip-trip-trip, while I watched her with this tight steel band round my chest.

I could never bear to think about the kid, and I couldn't now; lying in that cradle, completely helpless, brought into the world by mistake. I thought, why didn't I marry her? Why did I run away? And then it became, why did I run away? because marrying wouldn't have worked, I knew that, really; even at times like this, awake in the dark. I hadn't loved her.

But I shouldn't have run away; I was in two minds about it, right to the very moment of getting on the plane. At the bottom of the steps, on the tarmac, I'd actually turned round, I was going back. Then a man bumped into me from behind and I kept on going, like an ant in a column; once you're in the column, that's it, and perhaps that's why I'd put myself there.

In Mallorca, I'd gone wild, I'd screwed and I'd drunk and I'd swum, and I'd burned myself black on the beach, trying to get that picture out of my mind, the baby's face in the cradle; which was the picture that had driven me away. I knew I couldn't bear to see it again, it tore me apart; what it said was, marry her or go, and I'd gone, I couldn't marry her. But then I'd never marry Audrey, who I *wanted* to marry, and if I did, I knew it would be hell, the sort of hell she must have given her husband.

Except, of course, that she never found him attractive; a little, kind, ugly man in a family merchant bank. I was still making love to her, on and off, the four years she was married; in fact, that was one of the best times. She hated him so much she'd got none left for me. People called her a gold digger, especially after the divorce went through and she got all that money, but I knew it wasn't as simple as that; that she loathed herself for having married him, and hated him because of it; but something in her needed the money and the security, while something else despised her for needing it. I didn't know. It was too complex for me.

What I could still do was something for the kid; I didn't even know his name. I'd thought about it before, but now I'd do it, I'd get in touch with her, I'd find out where he was—I didn't have to see him—and I'd ... But that was where it stopped; it always did. I'd do what? Pay for his education? I'd got no money; an architect would have more money than I had. Help him, encourage him? How could I, when they wouldn't let me see him? And so round it went, round and round, until the pill worked and I fell asleep, and woke up feeling just the same, wishing I was dead, knowing everything was hopeless.

CHAPTER TWO

Jane phoned me at about nine o'clock. She said, 'You *do* sound miserable.' I said, 'I'm not awake, yet.' She said, 'Someone's given me two tickets for a play at the Saville, tonight; do you want to come?' I said, 'What is it?' and she said, 'I'm not sure, I think it's a French play,' and I thought, oh, Jesus. I was going to tell her no, I just couldn't make it, but I changed my mind, at least it filled the evening, because in moods like these, I lose initiative, I won't go out, I won't ring anybody, least of all a bird, so I said, 'Yes, okay, I'll come.'

In fact it wasn't a French play, she'd got it wrong, as usual; it was an American comedy, set in Paris. I wasn't in the mood for comedy, and this one wasn't even funny. It was full of English actors trying to put on phoney American accents, and old-fashioned double takes, and people going through the wrong bedroom doors. The only thing that interested me at all was that one of the boys had been at RADA with me. He wasn't bad, at least his accent was a bit more authentic than the others', but watching him play the part he'd been stuck with, I felt glad I'd got out of the theatre; weeks and weeks hanging about on the dole, and when you got a part it was something like this, which might fold up in a fortnight; or, even worse, go on for a couple of years.

Afterwards, at dinner, Jane said, 'Geoff, you *must* finish your play. Honestly, if a play like that can get on.' I told her, 'Dozens of plays like that get on. It's a commercial play.' She said, 'But yours is so much funnier; *and* set in England. It would mean more to people.' I patted her on the hand and said, 'It's not people, it's managements,' and she said, 'Well them, as well.' I changed the subject, she was irritating me; because to tell the truth, I *had* been thinking about my own play while I watched the other, thinking, Christ, if this sort of rubbish gets on ... But hearing *her* talk about it made it sound ridiculous, a kind of parody of me.

We were in an Indian restaurant near the theatre, and another thing that was getting at me was I knew I wouldn't have enough money to pay, which would mean borrowing from her, and worse than that I knew it wouldn't surprise her, that she'd shame me, she'd take out her handbag and say, 'How much, darling?' not even expecting to get it back; Jesus, how different from Audrey.

And she said it, 'How much, darling?' 'Could you manage a couple of quid, darling?' Only her darling was the real thing and mine was the theatrical darling, meaning bugger all, otherwise I couldn't have said it. Still, it made her happy. I looked at her and wished to God I could be in love with her. Why not? People often were. There was a fellow called Vincent, a photographer, who was nuts about her; he'd sometimes ring her up while I was at her flat, and then he got the treatment that I supposed she got from me: 'No, Vincent, I can't see you tomorrow. No, I can't possibly manage next Monday either. All right: Saturday afternoon, then, but just for an hour.'

In a way it consoled me; at least, if she wanted him, she'd got somebody, and if I was giving her the run around, she was giving it to him. In fact that seemed to be life, that was how it went, in a nasty little circle; Jane and the photographer, me and Jane, Audrey and me. It all seemed such a bloody waste.

33

I'd met him once, when I'd called for her at the flat. She'd obviously had him on for the afternoon, me for the evening, and I'd turned up early, or else he'd stayed late. I felt sorry for him, she was so obviously keen to get rid of him, and he was so apologetic, so quick to take the hint and get out. He was a gentle sort of guy, very quiet, quite good-looking, too, with a long, straight nose, and brown wavy hair. When he'd gone I wanted to say to her, 'Look, *he's* your type, not me. Stick to him, marry him, have children, he'll look after you, I'll only make you unhappy.' But of course she'd only have been insulted, just like I was when Audrey did the same to me.

So I just said, 'He seems quite nice,' and she'd said, 'Oh, Vincent's all right, I suppose, but he's so boring, he's so indecisive. I can do whatever I like with him.'

She looked pretty in the restaurant, tonight; she'd obviously had her hair done that afternoon and she smiled and her eyes shone, and her dress was cut low, so I could see the nice, smooth, round tops of her breasts; I wanted to reach out and stroke them. She saw me looking and it made her happy; she reached across the table and squeezed my hand. Hers was very warm; I left mine there as long as I could, then pulled it away, and her smile went, she'd been hurt again; and so it went on.

To make up for it, I said yes, I'd go back to her flat for coffee. She said, 'Marion will probably be in bed.' In a way I hoped she would, in another I didn't; it would be easier to escape, if she was up; I didn't want to stay the night.

And she was up, she was in the sitting-room with her boy-friend, a middle-aged clot who'd left his wife but hadn't been divorced by her, and who couldn't stand the sight of me, which was mutual. They were obviously furious to see us, they'd probably been settling down to some heavy petting, and Marion slept in this room.

34

Marion said, 'I'll make some more coffee,' as if it was arsenic, and flounced out of the room. Her boy-friend, Naughton, looked at me and asked, 'How are all the talking dogs?' This was a reference to a commercial I'd worked on about a year ago, two bloodhounds and a bowl of dog food, and he'd run the thing into the ground ever since he'd known I'd made it.

I said, 'Wonderful. Changed any good number plates lately?' He went all huffy at once and said, 'Every car we sell comes straight from the factory, whether it's a Rolls or a Ferrari. I rather thought that was generally known.' He was tall and thin, pink in the face from the amount he drank, with popping grey eyes, and a grey ring of hair; it made him seem older than he was. Jane thought he looked distinguished; I thought he just looked clapped out.

We glared at each other, then he picked up the evening paper and pretended to read it. Jane looked at him then looked at me and shrugged; I think he rather fancied her, which was part of the trouble. When Marion brought in the coffee, Jane tried to beat up conversation; what the play had been like, how I'd seen someone in it I knew, that sort of jazz, while Naughton kept turning pages of the paper, and Marion practically froze us out. I thought, oh, to hell with it, I'm going home, and started to get up, but when I did that, Jane got desperate, she took the coffee cup out of my hands and said, 'I'll pour you some more,' then made a face at Marion, pointing at Naughton, still behind the paper. Marion just raised her eyebrows, meaning, what can *I* do? and it didn't worry me; I'd no wish to talk to the pig.

But the end of it was I had to; Jane lured him out by offering him a cup of coffee, too. He grunted at her, very graciously, but he had to drop the paper. For my own part, I'd have been happier if he'd stayed there; there wasn't a thing we didn't disagree on, politics, sex, religion, art, and if we didn't disagree, it worried me. It was his damned pontifical way of saying things that really got me; with a little pleased smile, to tell you he felt sorry for you, being so ignorant as to disagree. Marion sat there parroting, yessing everything he said. Jane was always telling me how kind she was, how sweet and generous, but I could never see it. To me she seemed sour, as jealous as hell — particularly of Jane — and a bloody snob into the bargain. She was thirty-one, and she loathed not being married, but if she ever was, I felt sorry for the man she got; she'd crush him like a boa constrictor. I suppose she wasn't too bad-looking, Jane was always on about how beautiful her eyes were — they were big and grey — but her nose was too big and her mouth was the give-away, turned down and discontented. She dyed her hair blonde, which didn't suit her, and she had some *very* responsible job as a personnel officer somewhere; another of the legends was that she was 'wonderful with people'.

She said, 'Well, tell us about the play, then,' and Jane said, 'It was rather feeble, wasn't it, Geoff?' I said, 'Yes, I suppose so.' Whenever I found myself confronted by those two, I'd go back into my shell like a tortoise, it was the only way. Jane said, 'It was an American play,' and Naughton said, 'Oh, *well*,' which nettled me immediately. I said, 'What do you mean, oh well?' He said, 'The American sense of humour is adolescent,' as if he'd discovered some great, shattering truth. I said, 'They'd probably say the same about us, if they came over here and saw *Worm's Eye View* and *Salad Days*.'

Marion said, 'I liked *Salad Days*,' which laid her wide open, but I let it pass, I said, 'And a lot of people probably liked this play, tonight.' Naughton said, 'Yes; adolescents.'

That got me. I said, 'But *Salad Days* is for sophisticates.' Jane tried to change the subject, but Naughton said, '*Salad Days* doesn't pretend to be anything but what it is.

The trouble with American humour is it has this layer of sophistication, but underneath it's quite ingenuous.'

Marion said, 'Just like American men. They all put up this great façade, but once it drops, they're just a lot of little mother's boys.' I said, 'I imagine you've had a wide experience.' She said, 'I worked there as a secretary for a year. I travelled right across the country,' and Naughton gave me a that-puts-*you*-in-your-place look. I said. 'Well, perhaps that makes me an adolescent, too,' which brought a great, big smirk from him, but I let it go, it wasn't worth arguing.

After that, we played out this pantomime; he and Marion wanting to get us out so they could go to bed together, Jane wanting to get me into the bedroom next door, and all of them going through the act that we could sit here talking the whole night. As for me, I just wanted to go home, and as soon as it looked as if I would—if I moved or yawned or glanced at my watch—Marion and Naughton would brighten up, and Jane would fly into a panic and get me another drink or start on a new tack of conversation. In the end, she managed it rather neatly, she suddenly came out with, 'That reminds me! I want you to see my new rocking chair, Geoff. Would you excuse us?' and carted me off to her room.

When we were there, among all the glass cats and china ornaments and coloured cushions, she said, 'I *am* sorry, darling.' I said, 'Doesn't matter. Not your fault.' I was wondering how I could get out of there, now she'd got me in. I sat down in the rocking chair and started rocking. She said, 'Just as well I thought of it, wasn't it? I got it last week in the Portobello Road; I think it's Victorian.' I said, 'Very nice,' and she said, 'You'll stay, won't you?' looking at me with great, wide eyes, bursting with pathos, I'll die if you don't say yes, so I said, 'Yes, okay, if you want me to,' which was as gracious as I could make it,

37

and all that she wanted. She said, 'You know I always want you to.'

So I stayed, I made love to her three times, while she made these *grateful* noises — oh-oh-*oh* — that always had a bad effect on me, they made me want to hurt her. I'd drive harder and harder, I'd bite her breasts or squeeze her buttock in my hand, but still she'd sound grateful, even if she was in pain. And then, right in the middle of everything, a thought came into my head; that while I was making Jane happy, Naughton was banging away at Marion, next door, like some factory; and I wanted to laugh, I only just turned it into a cough.

And God, I didn't envy Naughton. Lying beside Jane afterwards, with her fingers on my cock, hardly moving, just expectant, I could imagine what it would be like: great, fleshy thighs and breasts, wanting more and more and more from the poor bastard; by the morning, he'd probably look like a death's head.

When I woke up, I was alone in the bed, I must have slept heavily; there was clattering and chinking from the kitchen, so I supposed breakfast was on the way; then, God help me, there was Marion's voice, singing, 'Oh, What A Beautiful Morning,' so I supposed it had gone all right; at least for her.

Jane brought the breakfast in on a tray and gave it me in bed, like she always did, when I stayed. She said, 'Naughton's gone,' and I said, 'Leaving a satisfied customer.' She made a face, but couldn't help herself laughing; for once. Then she sat on the bed and ran her fingers down my cheek; I hated that when I was eating, my natural reaction was to switch her off like a horse, but I stopped it. And yet at the same time I felt grateful to her, the misery had lifted, I could face things, now. If only she wouldn't go just that little bit too far, ask just that little bit too much; like now, when she said, 'You do make me

38

happy,' waiting for, 'And you make *me* happy,' except I couldn't say it. I stuck the eggspoon in my mouth and grunted, and she got up from the bed and said, 'I'll have to get ready, darling. You can leave when you like.'

I didn't get up till she'd gone, Marion had gone before her; then I had a bath, shaved with Jane's tiny little golden razor, dressed, and went pottering round the flat, which is a bad habit of mine in other people's places. I knew Jane's room; what interested me was Marion's, the sitting-room. It was full of kitsch, fluffy things, woolly animals, and on the sofa, the divan bed where she slept, a great, pink teddy bear.

I picked it up and looked at it; it was old, which surprised me even more: she'd obviously had it for years. The fur was worn and moth-eaten, almost as if it was going grey; one of the button eyes was missing, you could see she'd probably had it from childhood, and I just didn't get it. It didn't seem to go with all her practicality, her down-to-earthness and no-nonsense, the sort of advice I kept hearing she'd been giving Jane, especially about me; cut your losses, face the facts, pull yourself together.

I still had the thing in my hand when the key turned in the front-door lock; I just had time to drop it and skip across the room when Marion came in. She said in the voice she usually put on for me—very cold and flat—'Hallo, still here?' Then her eyes went straight across the room, almost like a mother's to a child, and she saw the teddy bear, sprawled, not sitting up, now, on the sofa; she gave me a really vicious look, I might have killed it; she really hated me. I said, 'Forgotten something?' She said, 'Yes, a file,' she spat it out, and something came over me, I said, 'Not the teddy bear?'

She didn't answer at first, she went over to the sofa and sat the thing up, I could swear that she patted its head, then she said, 'Haven't you any sense of decency?' I said,

'Yes, of course I have.' She said, 'There's my desk, over there. Why don't you go through the drawers? Or perhaps you have,' and I gave a little laugh, I couldn't believe it, I said, 'Steady on, Marion.'

She snatched down the file from one of the bookshelves, and came striding back across the room. I asked very quietly, 'Marion; why don't you like me?' and she stopped and gave me her lower-than-dirt look, again. She said, 'Because you're vulgar and spineless, and you treat Jane appallingly.'

I said, 'I know I'm vulgar. I can't help it. It's my background.' For a moment that took the wind out of her sails, then she said, 'And you revel in it, don't you?' I said, 'Do I? What would you prefer me to do? Cover it up?' which pulled her up short again. She made as if to go, then changed her mind and said, 'Why can't you leave Jane alone?' I said, 'Me?' She said, 'Yes, you; it's in *your* hands.'

I said, 'You don't know what you're talking about. What can I do, when she's on the phone to me, day after day; let's go there, please come here?' She said, 'And you fall in with it, don't you?' I said, 'Rubbish.' She said, 'Yes, you do; when it suits you. When you're short of somebody to go to bed with, or you want someone's lap to cry on.' I said, 'You've really made a study of me, haven't you?' She said, 'It's not too difficult.' I said, 'You wouldn't say you were jealous of her?' She said, 'With *you?*' She really spat it at me; it wasn't what I'd meant, but seeing her now I thought, Christ, maybe it *is* true.

She said, 'I only get involved with adult men.' I said, 'Of course. Like Naughton.' She said, 'He's worth ten of you. He's more of a man than you'll ever be.' I said, 'I'm sure he is,' perhaps I smiled, because she jumped on me again. She said, 'He's mature and responsible ... ' I said, 'And he doesn't cry in your lap. *I* know.'

We just stood looking at each other, then, till she said, 'Just for once in your life, do something unselfish. Think of what this is doing to Jane,' and that was her exit line.

I sat down on the divan, beside the teddy bear, and did some thinking. I hate rows, and you could tell she thrived on them. That stuff about vulgarity was what you'd have expected from her, with her snobbishness, and anyway, I knew what I was, I didn't need her to tell me; I knew how I sounded, and it didn't worry me; she could stuff her Oxford accents, especially the awful braying noise that Naughton made. As for Jane and me, what the hell did she know about it? Be unselfish, leave her alone; it was all so one-sided. I'd tried, for God's sake; it was like getting rid of a limpet. If I didn't see her, I made her unhappy, and if I did see her, I made her unhappy.

What really made me laugh was the picture Marion had of Naughton, the great tower of strength, the he-man. All she meant was that he treated her like shit—I knew it from Jane—but you'd only got to look at him and listen to him, God help you, for an evening to get his number. Talk about laps to cry in; though you couldn't say there wasn't enough of Marion's to go round.

I put on my coat and left, I wished to Christ I'd never stayed, I hadn't wanted to; Marion and Naughton at night, and Marion on her own in the morning: Jesus! I'd keep well away in the future, if there was any bedding to be done, it would have to be done at my place.

When I got outside, the square cheered me up a bit; all those tall, neat Regency houses and the garden in the middle, you couldn't believe you were in Islington. Then you drove out into the main road and you knew you were; noise and bloody supermarkets with placards all over the window and ugliness and mods and rockers everywhere.

I drove down Upper Street, back into town; I had an appointment with the managing director of an agency at eleven. He was one I liked; not that he didn't put on a front, but the one he put on was different from all the others. They were sleeker than sleek, he was shaggier than shaggy; they were smooth and he was blunt. I suppose in some ways he was a bigger fraud than they were, because if you were going to be in advertising, you might as well do it properly, with the 'old boy' touch, the hand on the shoulder and the buttoned-down collars and the sixty-guinea suits and the phoney integrity, as if all of it mattered like hell.

The first thing this chap said to me when I came into his office—it was in Cockspur Street—was, 'Why the hell don't you go back on the stage?'

I said, 'You know why; because I'm no bloody good.' He liked that sort of answer. He said, 'Sheer idleness, that's all; you know how much easier it is to make a living scribbling slogans. Anyway, at least you're honest about it. Not like my copywriters, still kidding themselves they're going to write a great novel when they're thirty-five, and they can't even turn out decent copy.'

This was another bit of his: that anyone outside advertising had to be better than anybody in it, which was all right with me. Now and again he'd try to persuade me to come and work for him full time, but not too seriously; I got the feeling that he wanted me to refuse, and when I did, he'd say, 'Don't blame you, don't blame you,' and obviously think the more of me for it.

He was about fifty-five, tallish and grey and a bit scraggy, with a moustache. You got the impression he'd been an officer in the war, probably a colonel of some sort, and he'd given up using the rank but still kept the manner.

He said, 'Don't mind if I take my coat off, do you? So damned hot in here,' as if the office had nothing to do with him. He stood up, tugged off his jacket, and slung it on a chair, all part of the act, then he said, 'We've just got the Dougall's Whisky account,' very throw-away, such a damn nuisance. 'Came to us from Porterhouse and Price; they want a new image.' He pushed a couple of designs across the desk at me; one of them was a flying whisky bottle, Dougall's, with wings like a bird; the other was a whisky bottle bobbing about in the ocean. He said, 'Bit coy?'

I made a face that might have meant anything; he could be touchy at times. He said, 'Had a few captions written for them; I don't think any of them's any damn good. Look, take them away and see if they strike any sparks from you. If they don't, just bring them back.' I said, 'All right.' You never talked about money with him, that was something he liked to raise himself; or rather, fling out suddenly, as if it embarrassed him. As I got to the door, he said, 'Seventy-five consultation fee. More, if we use your stuff.' I said, 'Fine,' and he gave a stiff little nod, then looked down at the papers on his desk. Dismissed.

When I got out in the street, I practically skipped along. Seventy-five quid! Jesus! The things I could do with that! I was right out of trouble. I'd got all my confidence back; I wanted to ring Audrey and say come to lunch, come to dinner, till I remembered she was in Paris. So I drove down to the Kings Road and bought myself a black suede jacket, one of the new kind without lapels. I bought a pair of shoes as well—black, no laces, elastic-sided—then I had lunch at the Casserole.

And *she* was there. I didn't notice her at first; the lighting's quite dim, even in the daytime. In fact what told me she was there was her laugh, you could never mistake it, very high and clear and nervous; the big thing about her that always used to infuriate me. I heard it just as I was beginning on my smoked salmon; she was right across the room with her back to me, thank God, and she couldn't have seen me come in; or perhaps she had, and hadn't spoken. The man with her was very smooth, forty or so, dressed to the nines in a sharp grey suit, a pink striped shirt, one of those black, knitted ties, and a lot of hair all over the place, most of it going grey. I seemed to have seen him around at parties, or maybe it was just someone like him; there were dozens. I heard him say in the sort of affected voice you'd expect, 'Of course, it all depends what one *wants* from television.'

Right away, I couldn't eat. I thought, my typical bloody luck, a good thing happens, then *this*. Once, she turned round and I ducked my head. I just caught a glimpse of her; still very pretty, but worn, too much make-up—she'd always been prone to that, lashing on rouge and eye shadow.

I didn't even finish what I'd got on my fork, I put it down when it was halfway to my mouth; all I wanted to do was get out before she saw me. The waiter came over and said, 'Don't you like it? *We* thought it was rather nice.' I said, 'It *is* nice, it's me, I seem to have got indigestion. Can I have the bill?' He said, 'Of *course*,' and floated off, and she must have heard my voice, because she turned round again and this time looked at me.

We held it for a second or two, neither of us spoke, then she turned away. Looking at me, she'd had no real expression. Surprised, perhaps, but more ... expectant, have it *your* way, recognise me and I'll recognise you, talk to me and I'll talk to you. The one thing I'd been afraid of was, '*Ha*-llo, Geoff,' and a lot of frothy, phoney conversation, like that other time in the Kings Road.

So I paid my bill and got out; she didn't look up as I went past her table. In fact, out of the corner of my eye, I saw her look down; she seemed to be frowning.

Driving home, I thought what a bloody village London was, you couldn't escape people; and yet if there was someone you really wanted to see, some girl, especially, it was a million to one you'd never bump into them. For example, Audrey; I'd never yet run across her, without fixing it, and I knew I never would. If I ever did manage to break clear of her, there'd be none of those 'Fancy meeting you' things to start it up again.

CHAPTER THREE

That Sunday was the first in the month, so I went to see my parents, in Harringay. I never liked going but I owed it them, not just the family thing, but they'd been decent to me in the past; once or twice, when I'd been broke, they'd let me come back and live at home.

My father opened the front door when I pulled up outside, and came down the path, to the gate. He said, 'Running all right now, is it?' I said, 'Yes, not bad, still a bit of trouble with the ignition.' Cars were something we could talk about; we talked about them quite a lot.

He unlatched the gate and said, 'Mother's in the kitchen.' She usually was. He was a big man, bigger than me, with the same wiry hair—he'd kept it all, though it was going grey—and a grey moustache. He still talked with a Devon accent, though he'd left Paignton over thirty years ago, and he still kept this house, semi-detached, though he'd been making a lot more money since the war.

I said, 'George here?' That was my brother who worked with him, building, but he said, 'No, playing golf,' which was all right with me. George was older than I was, and we'd never got on. He'd been the good boy who'd gone into the business, married a *nice* girl, had a couple of kids, but there was something gnawing at him, something he seemed to think he'd missed and I'd got. Girls, maybe; I don't know. I think he had this picture of me, something that went back to when we were both still at home; man about town, in and out of bed all day, no responsibilities.

46

He didn't know I often envied *him*; a life that ran itself, responsibilities that didn't vary, instead of problems that were changing all the time.

I think there was another thing; I was meant to be the 'favourite', my mother's, anyway. I sensed it there, but again, he'd never said so, not since schooldays; he never said much, in any case. Perhaps it was true, God knows, but what did it matter, now? It was all dead history.

I went through the hall, past the front room with all that shining mahogany and hideous china, into the kitchen, where she was, beside the stove. If I could have painted her, that was where she'd have been standing.

She said, '*Ha*-llo, darling!' and came and kissed me. I gave her a hug; she'd put on weight the last few years, always stocky and square, but now she'd slowed up quite a bit. She said, 'Found a nice girl?' That was always the joke, though underneath, I don't think it was one. I said, 'You know I can't find anyone as nice as you,' which was my stock reply, and she said, 'Get on with you!' She said, 'You know your father gave up his fishing today to see you; two of his friends were going,' and I said, 'You shouldn't have done that, Dad; why didn't you ring and tell me?'

He said, 'No, no; fair's fair; first Sunday in the month,' but just a little smugly. You could always tell when he thought he was making a sacrifice; you were meant to. I tried to feel guilty or appreciative or something, but I couldn't. I'd always hated his damned fishing, ever since I was a kid and he'd drag me along, to sit on the banks of miserable brown rivers in the rain, or prick my fingers fixing bait on to his hooks, or wait for ever in his stuffy car, outside pubs.

My mother said, 'Well, what have you got to tell us?' and as usual I struggled to think; what *had* I got to tell them, or rather, what had I got that I *could* tell them? I

47

said, 'Oh, nothing much. I've been working on copy for some whisky advertisements.' My father said, 'That sounds all right. Get any free samples?' and Mother said, 'Don't listen to him, he gets enough as it is, him and his Rotarians.'

He was wearing the Rotary badge now, sometimes I thought he put it in his pyjama button-hole and slept in it. God, the Rotarians; the fishermen and the Rotarians, the fishermen who *were* Rotarians. When they came to the house, I'd run for cover.

I said, 'And then there's this children's book, the one I'm doing with John,' and Mother said, 'Oh, you didn't tell us about that,' so I told them about that, for the second or third time; at least it got us into the dining-room and halfway through lunch; then Dad went off on one of his fishing stories, and I put on my fishing-story face. I'd perfected it over the years, glassy-eyed attention, you couldn't tell it from the real thing. The only problem was to know when he'd finished and say the right thing, but after a time I'd got good at that, as well. It was instinctive; something in the cadence, something in his expression; triumph, perhaps, he always came out on top. And then, when the moment came, I'd say, 'Go on?' or, 'Did you really?' or, 'I'll be damned,' perm any one from three.

This particular story was about a pike or a carp, I wasn't sure which, or maybe about a pike that got in among the carp, I don't know. Anyway, the old man came out on top at the end, like he always did, gaffing the pike or catching the carp, or whatever.

After lunch, thank God, there was a B.B.C. programme he wanted to see, some football match — 'We only watch commercial in case there's something of yours on, Geoff,' another hardy annual. The television was in the sitting-room; Mother and I sat just behind him, in leather arm-chairs, and now and again she'd whisper to me. Just questions about how was I keeping, how was I eating, who

48

was doing my laundry, all skirting round the ones she really wanted to ask, and I didn't want to answer: 'Are you in love? Who are you going with? When will you marry her?'

I always felt uncomfortable in the sitting-room, she'd made it into my trophy room; photographs of me on the stage, certificates, even the RADA gold medal; there it was in a glass case on the wall, sending me up, reproaching me. I sometimes wished I'd never let them have it, just thrown it away and told them it got lost. Still, I knew what it meant to them, it was a sort of reassurance; that once upon a time I'd got it, so who could tell, maybe whatever it was was still there? I knew they'd been upset when I chucked acting—just as they'd been a bit choked when I took it up. But then they'd come to terms with it, at least it was something they could plug into; the gold medal and seeing me on a stage, and now—here I was, drifting again.

You couldn't blame them, they were simple people, they wanted tangible things. A house going up was something you could see; so was a name on a marquee. But what the hell was a ten-second telly commercial? It took something bigger than an M.G. to persuade you you could touch *that*.

I knew the party line, now; I was 'in advertising', but I'd heard the tone of voice when they said it. If I got married, that was something they could latch on to, again, especially Mother; daughter-in-law and grandchildren and all that, just like she could with George. If I got married, I might 'settle down'. That was very important to them, settling down, it meant you didn't worry them any more.

There was the usual big tea, scones and jam and home-made cake and all that jazz; I could hardly touch it after all the roast beef and Yorkshire; they always seemed to

49

think they had to feed me enough to get me through the month. Mother kept saying, '*Try* the cake,' and I'd plough my way through another slice of it.

When I left, she came to the front door and put her arm round my shoulders; she said, 'Bring us some good news!' I knew what she meant.

That night, I went to a party in one of those posh blocks near Baker Street; given by an account executive I knew. He wasn't married, I don't think he was even queer; I don't know what the hell he was. He was thin and cold, like a fish, with shiny black hair, a long, white face, and a tiny, black moustache that I could never quite believe; a Chaplin moustache. The only thing you could definitely say about him was that he was ambitious. Yet even then, he never gave you any bullshit about the function of advertising, like some of them did, or the merits of his product; he just moved on and on, I suppose towards bigger and better offices, bigger and better desks; certainly not to bigger and better secretaries. Simply to more and more money, though God knows what he'd do with it, when he got it.

You only had to look round the flat to see he'd no idea how to spend it. The place had nothing to do with him at all; he'd obviously asked somebody who was the okay interior decorator, given him his head, and the decorator had gone mad: white, rough-cast walls, a blue-and-white terrazzo floor, black leather sofas, and those big, thick, sticky, touch-me paintings. He seemed to move around it in a kind of daze, 'Is this me?' There was a hi-fi playing cool West Coast stuff, which wasn't remotely him, either.

One or two couples were dancing, but most of them were standing around in corners, drinking and chatting. He came up to me and said, 'Hallo, Geoff, I'm glad you could come.' This was the nice thing about him, he always did seem really pleased to see you, though there was something a bit pathetic about it, too; as though he was surprised that anyone he invited actually came—and even a sort of appeal; as if *you* were the only one who might help him get out of himself. I had this funny feeling that he wanted me to go round introducing him to his own guests.

He said, 'May I offer you a drink?' His manners always made me feel like a lout. I wondered, like I always did when I met him, what the hell he was doing in advertising at all, when every stroke he took must have been against the current. He was way further out than all the little twerps who thought they were really too good for it because now and then they had a poem read on the Third Programme.

I said, 'Fine, yes,' and he got me a whisky. There was none of this bloody champagne cup stuff at his parties.

My eye was travelling round the room; ad men, telly men, and some very nice birds; slim, expensive birds with jazzy hair-dos and backless dresses. Bill took me up to one of them, her hair was dyed a silver blonde, and she was standing in a corner by a bookshelf with hardly a book in it—I suppose the decorator hadn't thrown any in. She was talking to a gawky woman in diamanté glasses, who I knew was some sort of female journalist, and a squattish man in a blue suit with a bright red face and very close curled fair hair. Bill said, 'Mr and Mrs Janes and Miss Grimes.' The blonde smiled at me, and I wished it hadn't been her husband. He asked in a high, rather peevish, voice, 'Are you in advertising, too?'

I said, 'Yes, sort of,' but he wouldn't let it go, he said, 'What does "sort of" mean?' I said, 'It means I write advertising copy, but not in an agency.' The Grimes woman said, 'Freelance,' and the man said, 'Isn't that a little precarious?' and I thought, oh, *Christ*. I said, 'No, why should it be?' The stupid tit. He said, 'I only meant there must be more security if you're working in an agency.' I said, 'There is,' and let it go; there was a silence then, which I'd meant there to be, then the Grimes woman jumped in with something tactful about freelance work giving more variety, and the silver blonde said, 'Oh, *much* more,' and I realised she was *for* me; or perhaps just not for him.

I asked him, 'What do *you* do?' and he said, 'Plastics,' very quickly, as if it embarrassed him. I said, 'I suppose you use Bill's agency.' He said, 'As a matter of fact, we do.' Then he started asking questions about advertising again; how did you get ideas, did you *believe* in the products you worked on, and I got annoyed with the way it was drifting, this identifying me with advertising—you advertising people—when to me it was just a way to make money; as soon as I found a better way, I'd give it up.

He said, 'But how do you begin? Did you always want to go into advertising?' I said, 'As a matter of fact, I was on the stage.' I hadn't meant to let it out, but he'd needled me; I knew the endless, stupid questions I'd be in for, now. Still, his wife said, 'On the *stage*,' in a hushed, holy voice, so I was almost glad I had. He gave her a nasty little jab of a look and said, 'That's very interesting,' as though I'd told him I'd done time for rape. 'On the London stage? Perhaps we've seen you. We go a great deal.'

I said, 'I don't suppose you did; I only did a couple of things in the West End, and neither of them ran for long.' She said, 'What were they?' She'd come to life, and you could see he didn't like it. I said, 'A Coward revival at the Garrick, and a play called *Windfall* at the Lyric, Hammersmith.' He laughed and said, 'That's not quite West End,' but she said, 'I think I saw that!' She got quite excited. 'Wasn't it set in Cornwall, or somewhere? About a farmer's family.' I said, 'That's right. I was in love with my mother.'

Her husband said, 'It sounds like kitchen sink,' and I said, 'Not kitchen sink; cattle trough.' She obviously wanted to talk about it, but he cut across her, he said, 'What made you leave the theatre?' which I'd known was coming. I said, 'I got tired of acting.' They said, 'Tired of *acting*? Tired of *ac*ting?' I said, 'Yes.' She said, 'How can anyone get tired of acting?' and he said, 'Oh, I can understand it. It's an artificial sort of life.' I got annoyed, then, I said, 'No more artificial than advertising — or plastics.'

He said, 'I'll grant you *ad*vertising,' and his wife said, 'Oh, darling, there's no comparison. Acting's an art.' He said, 'How *does* one get tired of acting?' and I shrugged, I wished to Christ he'd belt up. If I did find the answer, he'd never understand it.

His wife said, 'I'd love to be able to act. I'd never get tired of acting.' I said, 'One does,' and *he* leaped in, saying, 'Yes, I can see it. After all, an actor's really a puppet, isn't he? Even a great actor like Olivier; he's still dancing to someone else's tune.' The Grimes woman chimed in, then, and I let her get on with it; I didn't want to talk to him. Once or twice I caught a glance from his wife, and I wondered how I could isolate her, it would probably mean breaking away, then coming back, unless I asked her to dance, and on the spur of the moment I did, I thought, fuck him, and I said, 'Like to dance?'

She smiled and said, 'Yes, love to,' and off we went; his mouth drew tight, he was livid, for a moment he stopped talking, but by the time we'd moved out and I looked round, he was talking, again.

She said, 'You mustn't mind Guy, he's always probing at people.' She had a very nice smile, warm and humorous, she looked the sort of girl who'd laugh a lot: not giggle. In fact she was very pretty; the nearer you got to her, the more you appreciated it; large grey eyes, a thin, straight nose, and a rather wide mouth. She pressed against me

53

very gently as we danced, not enough for anyone to notice, but enough to show it wasn't by accident.

I said, 'Questions like that drive me up the wall, I'm afraid,' and she laughed and said, 'I could see that.' Her arms were very smooth and brown and slim; I wanted to run my hands up and down them. I said, 'Can I telephone you?' She said, 'We're in the book; Guy Janes, Colebrook Court.' I said, 'Fine,' and she suddenly looked anxious, she said, 'You'll remember that? Colebrook Court.'

I phoned her next day. She said, 'You!' as if she was surprised, and I said, 'Why, who were you expecting?' She laughed and she said, 'Oh, no one in particular,' and I said, 'Well, that's who I am. No one in particular.' She laughed again and said, 'I don't believe you're really so modest.'

We met for lunch in a Chinese restaurant in South Kensington, not far from where she lived. She laughed a lot, and when I touched her knee with mine, under the table, she didn't move it away. There was something very restless about her, I could sense it; she kept talking about things she wanted to do, things she wanted to see, places she wanted to go: New York, Athens, Moscow, even India. She said, 'If only *I'd* been able to act: it isn't fair!' She tried to paint, she said, and she made her children toys—'I'm afraid that's the only way I'm a good mother'—and she was trying to learn Russian. She was obviously bored to death with her marriage, though when she talked about her husband, it was in a funny sort of apologetic way, as if she was a bit frightened of him, as if he was still strange to her. She said, 'Guy's terribly severe, Guy's very practical, Guy expects an awful lot from people,' obviously meaning herself. I didn't talk about him much, I find it's bad policy to talk to women about their husbands; they can say what they like, but if you join in, they get all guilty and defensive.

She said, 'How funny to find *you* at a party like that.' I said, 'Why?' and she said, 'Among all those advertising people. You're quite different from them. They're all so slick. And you … I don't know. You're like an actor.' I said, 'An ex-actor,' and she said, 'I'm sure you must have been good. Why did you really give up?' I said, 'I told you: I got tired of it,' and she shook her head, smiling at me.

I took her hand across the table, and she squeezed my fingers, hard. She said, 'You're bad for me. I must remember my responsibilities.'

After lunch, I drove her into town; she wanted to go shopping at Fenwick's. When I'd parked the car, I stroked her cheek with the back of my hand, and she looked at me very seriously, almost sadly, then I kissed her. She was very passionate; her tongue moved round and round in my mouth, and when she broke away, she said, 'I enjoyed that.' I kissed her again; this time I put my hand high up her thigh and squeezed it; she put hers over mine, but not to pull it away, to press it. She said, 'I think you're a very sensual young man.'

Two days later, she came to my flat. When I asked her to, she said, 'Is that wise?' I said, 'Why shouldn't it be?' and she said, 'Very well, I shall trust you.'

She was due at four. I sat there, wondering if she'd come, and if she did come, how late she'd be; I'd had so much of it from Audrey. But it was only five past four when the bell went, and there she was, in a dark-green coat, very elegant—smiling. She said, 'Hello!' and I drew her inside and kissed her. Then she stood back, with her hands on my shoulders, and said, 'Aren't you going to help me off with my coat?'

I did. Although it was cold outside, she was wearing a sleeveless dress, and now I was able to do what I'd wanted to; run my hands up and down her beautiful, smooth

55

arms. I said, 'What lovely arms you've got.' She said, 'They're too muscular; it's all that swimming,' then I put my hands over her breasts, small breasts but springy; she didn't push them away. Then we stood there, very quiet, I could hear her breathing, till she said, 'How many girl-friends have you got?'

I said, 'Me? None at all,' and she laughed and said, 'Liar! You've got dozens!' I said, 'None, none at all,' and pulled her back against me; I had an erection. She said, 'Oh, I like that,' and she relaxed in my arms.

I said, 'Let me show you the flat.' She said, 'You rotter, you mean the bedroom.' I said, 'That's part of the flat,' and turned her round and kissed her again. For a moment, she pulled her head back and said, 'I think I should go.' I said, 'No, no, don't go,' and went on kissing her; as I kissed her, I edged her down the passage, slowly, towards the bedroom. We went sideways through the open door-way, still kissing, till at last we tumbled over the bottom of the bed. She gave a little sigh, then, her eyes were shut, she seemed to be almost in a trance.

I slid my hand under her dress, down the front of her panties, and began to play with her. She gave a great, con-vulsive heave, then grabbed hold of my cock. With my left hand, I began unzipping her dress, but she didn't let me finish, she sat up with another jerk and pulled down the zip herself, ripped open another zip, hauled the dress over her head; one, two, three, like an automaton, threw it on to the floor, unhooked her bra, threw that on the floor as well, all in this furious haste.

I said, 'Let me, let me,' and rolled down her panties, taking her buttocks in my hands, lovely buttocks, small, but full and firm.

She made love in this same, frantic way, as if she hadn't had it for years and might not ever have it again, so there almost seemed more pain in it than pleasure. When she came, she arched her back, threshed about the bed, then pulled my head down to her, saying, 'Oh, you're wonderful!' and kissed me, biting at my tongue. I said, 'You've got a great body, Rosemary.' She said, 'So have you. Gorgeous. Strong,' and squeezed my ribs. I said, 'Fat, you mean.'

I rolled over so I was lying beside her; she ran her fingers through the hair on my chest. I felt happy but remote, floating nowhere, detached from everything; everybody. She said, 'I'd hate to fall in love with you.' I didn't answer; I just moved my hand over her pubic hair; there wasn't much of it, it was a dark blonde. She said, 'You're miles away, aren't you?' I said, 'No, I'm not. I heard you. Are you often in love?' She said, 'Oh, in fits and starts. Everything's like that, with me. I've no staying power.' I said, 'Neither have I.' She said, 'Haven't you? Are you a grasshopper, too? Is that why you gave up acting?' I said, 'No.' She said, 'Why *did* you?' but I turned to her and kissed her, her hand went straight to my cock, and then we were making love again.

It got cold in the room, and dark. Beside me, she was stretched out very white and still, like a statue on a tomb. I could smell her perfume, I didn't know its name, but I liked it; very delicate and subtle.

She shivered, then sat up. She said, 'Oh, God, it's late! I'll have to go!' I said, 'I'll put the fire on for you,' and she said, 'Yes, please!' and stood up by the bed, trembling, trying to look at her watch.

I went over and switched on the electric fire, then looked at my own; it was quarter to seven. She said, 'Oh, God, I'll get into such trouble!' I asked, 'What will you tell him?' She said, 'I don't know. I'll think of something, on the way. I'm not much good at camouflage; he always sees through it. He never says anything, he just looks at me.'

I drew the curtains, and switched on the bedside lamp.

57

She came to me and hugged me, with her head on my shoulder. She said, 'Oh, Geoff, what am I going to do about myself?' I thought, what the hell are any of us going to do? but I patted her shoulder, till at last she looked up and kissed me. She said, 'You know how I'd love to stay!'

She was in the bathroom when the phone went: Jane. I knew who it was before I answered it, and when I did, I somehow felt she guessed what was going on. She said, 'I bought two gorgeous avocado pears at lunchtime in Soho; would you like me to bring them over?' I said, 'Sorry, honey, I'm going out to dinner, otherwise I'd have loved it,' and I could see her face fall, just like her voice did, '*Oh.*' What the hell did she expect, giving me that much notice? I said, 'Look, can I phone you back later on or tomorrow or something? I've got John here, we're busy on the book,' which wasn't tactful, but was the first thing I thought of. She said, in a very flat voice, 'All right,' and I hung up.

When Rosemary came out of the bathroom she said, 'Who was that? Another of your girl-friends?' I said, 'Just someone from an agency.' She laughed and said, 'I bet!'

I offered to drive her home, but she said, 'No, a taxi's safer,' so I went downstairs with her, down to the main door, and kissed her. She said, 'That was lovely.'

When I got upstairs, I poured myself a whisky, then I thought, she must be back, and phoned Audrey. These were the best times to do it, after a fuck, when you didn't care, or cared a lot less; when you were relaxed, and she could hear it in your voice, instead of hearing the tension; how much you bloody well needed her.

She was there, as I'd guessed she would be; it was always the same. There was nothing unfairer in the world than love. I said, 'What were your impressions of the Post Impressionists?' She said, 'Who's that?' in a go on, amuse

58

me, voice. I said, 'Geoff,' and she said, 'You mean my Post Impressions.' I said, 'Your Last Post Impressions.' We were going like a bomb. She said, 'What have *you* been doing?' I said, 'Pining for you, of course.' It was the tone she liked, but it was only at times like these I could hit it. She laughed and said, 'I'm sure you were.' Usually there came a point when things got sticky, when I'd be putting off the moment to say, what are you doing? when can I see you? but in this mood I could just go chatting on.

So I told her about the whisky ads, I flogged it for more than it was worth, then about the kids' book, I said, 'I want to call it "The Adventures of a Camp Camel", which got a cheap laugh, then she went on about Paris and how dreary everyone there was, until *she* asked *me*, 'Are you doing anything tonight?' I said, 'Not that I *know* of, dear,' and she said, 'Come over, then, if you feel like it; I've got some people coming in for drinks.' Normally I'd have run a mile from that, because I'd been to enough of her 'evenings', full of 'interesting' people, pigs most of them, with me the only one who wasn't interesting.

This time when I got there she had a little queer photographer called Peter, who was always hanging around, a girl called Sara, red-haired and rather pretty, who worked in an art gallery, a morose sort of American called Dave, who was in television, and this French film director, who'd got a very exotic, Bardot-ish French bird with him, who was acting in the film he was making. That meant a lot of the conversation was in French, which was great when I understood about one word in three, which Audrey knew perfectly well.

So while they talked French, I drank. I saw Dave look at me quite sympathetically, once or twice, he was the best of them, and he was less bloody pretentious than most of her friends, even if he did talk a load of cod's wallop at times. But whenever I was in a group with her

59

like this, I'd start wondering; which of them have slept with her, which of them are sleeping with her, now, watching the way she looked at them, the way they looked at her, the way she laughed with them, listening for private jokes. She knew all this, of course, she got a kick out of it; now and again I'd catch her looking at *me*, with that cold little smile, and I suppose I must have looked pretty funny, sitting there, sullen and lowering. She'd said to me once, 'I love you in your jealous mood, you're all jowls; like a sulky bulldog.'

This evening, though, I was anaesthetised, or very nearly, and what the sex hadn't done, the alcohol did.

Of course, we got on to the art of the bloody film; Eisenstein and Fellini and James bloody Agee, whoever the hell he was. This was Dave's bit; he frowned and screwed up his face as though he was trying to give birth to some fabulous idea, and it looked all the stranger on him because he was an athletic type, not very tall but with a big head and heavy shoulders; you'd have expected him to be more interested in something like boxing.

Raymond, the French director, gave me a snotty look at one point and said, '*Monsieur ne s'intéresse pas du cinéma*,' which I got all right, and Audrey said, '*Il était acteur lui-même; très doué comme étudiant. Il a gagné la médaille d'or de l'Académie.*' She liked to surprise people, and he put on a real pantomime, eyebrows shooting up to his hairline, as if he couldn't believe it. '*Mais vraiment?*' Still, his bird started to look interested in me—which was something. I'd had a glance or two from her already. I said, 'That was a very long time ago,' and Raymond said, '*Ah, oui*,' as much as to say, so one gathers.

Dave shot me a quick, distracted sort of look—he was still wrestling with his great idea—and said, 'No, but Kafka's right; up to a *point*. The cinema does put the eyes in uniform, but is there anything wrong with uniform as *such?*' Peter came burbling in, '*I* should have said *every-thing*,' but Dave ignored him, he seemed to be wrapped up in an argument with himself. He said, 'Why shouldn't an artist use compulsion? He's concerned with the best way of communicating his images, whether it's with a pen, a paintbrush or a camera.' Raymond said, '*D'accord*,' and the film star gave his hand a little pinch; she was about as interested as I was.

This didn't stop Raymond going into a great spiel in French which I couldn't make head or tail of, apart from the catch phrases, *Cahiers du Cinéma*, *nouvelle vague* and the in names: Truffaut and Jean-Luc Godard and Antonioni. It seemed to me that whereas Dave, however involved he got, was really talking because the thing burned him up, Raymond was talking to show that Dave wasn't the only one who could philosophise.

I wondered where on earth the poor bloody actors came in. At times like this I used to think that we, or rather they, were just peasants, infantry, while the directors were generals telling them go here, go there, get shot at in this trench, go and sacrifice yourself on that barbed wire; that if the directors had their way, there wouldn't *be* any actors, only marionettes, robots, who couldn't answer back and always did what they were told.

And it was strange, I suddenly found myself feeling like an actor, again, getting quite resentful, thinking, where would you be without *us*? remembering the times I'd been in good casts which carried lousy directors. And if it was bad enough in the theatre, in the telly, what must it be like in cinema, where directors were God, where they chop films up in little bits, and shoot scenes when they feel like it.

And I was going to speak, I opened my mouth, I was going to ask, 'Where do actors come in?' but before I could get it out, Dave was off again, with something about the symbolism of *Last Year In Marienbad*, and in a way I

61

was relieved, because it wasn't my battle to fight; it had nothing to do with me, now.

As the night went on, I wondered how it was going to end, or how Audrey wanted it to end. Obviously Raymond couldn't stay, and Peter didn't count, so that left Dave and me. I'd have been quite happy for both of us to leave together, what with the afternoon, but I was afraid he'd stay when I went; I'd never been sure about him, whether it was an old thing that had sputtered out into just being friends—she was keen on that—or something that was still going on, or something that might go on, in the future. It was hard to tell from watching him, he was so turned in on himself, and hard, from watching Audrey. She smiled at him, but then she smiled at Peter; she talked about him in an amused way, saying he was clever but neurotic, but *I* amused her, too, and she slept with me.

At about midnight, Raymond and his French bird left; they were shooting next morning, at Pinewood. Then Sara got up and, to my surprise, Dave got up, too, saying, 'You're on my way home, I'll drop you.' That left me and the little, twittery photographer, and it was wonderful to sit there feeling no tension, not to be worried about him, not to be worried about myself, whether or not she'd have me, when in a way I almost hoped she wouldn't.

Peter entertained her, like a monkey on a stick; he was bitchy about everyone who'd gone. He said, 'You've got such *clever* friends, Audrey. All this marvellous theory, it makes me feel so unimportant; *I* just point the camera and take pictures. *Still* ones.' She said, 'Then you must develop a theory, Peter.' He said, 'Lovely! Will you help me? One of those gorgeous ones, full of long words no one can understand? Do you think I ought to use an alienation effect? What *is* an alienation effect? It always sounds like one of those dreadful doors other people go through at London Airport.' She said, 'That's for theatres, not cameras.' He said, 'Well, can't I be a *nouvelle vague* pho*tog*rapher?' And he gave an imitation of Raymond, quite a funny one, with the supercilious look and the gestures.

Audrey and I both laughed, and he went on to Dave, frowning and worrying, saying, 'Yeah, but Stanislavski didn't *mean* that.' Audrey said, 'You're malicious, Peter.' He said, 'Am I, dear? I don't *mean* to be. Perhaps it's just because I envy all these people their super theories.'

Audrey gave me a look. It said, isn't he comical? but with undertones, meaning, *we* know, don't we? putting him on the other side of the fence, telling *me* I was in, she wanted me to stay.

Peter didn't go till two o'clock, drinking and gossiping and clawing people, and when he did, I heard him, at the front door: 'Have *lots* of lovely fun.'

When she came back into the room, I was standing up, and walked towards her. Her face was quite changed now, not smiling any more; expectant, waiting. As I reached her, she lifted it to me, and I kissed her, and kissing her, close against her, I had an erection right away; I thought, thank God. I started to undress her there, in the middle of the sitting-room, and as I did, she opened my trousers and slipped her hand inside. I steered her very gently, more like just a hint, towards the door, but she shook her head, not speaking, and we made love where we were, on the carpet, calmly, not in the usual, frantic way she had, doing the things we knew the other wanted.

Afterwards, she lay on her back, her arms spread out wide and straight. I got up to finish my drink—it was still beside my chair—and she waved a hand at me, so I'd bring her hers. When we'd been drinking for a little, still in silence, she stretched her leg out and ran her toes down my thigh, giggling. I took her foot in my hand and squeezed it, and she drew in her breath; then, when I let

63

go, she moved it farther and farther up, till at last it was moving over my cock. She laughed again, and I rolled across the floor to her, to make love.

This time, when we'd finished, she got up and led the way into the bedroom; we lay there in bed, in each other's arms, still without a word, I don't think I've ever felt happier, till at last she said, 'Why aren't you always like this?' I said, 'Like what?' though I guessed what she meant. She said, 'You know.' How could I answer that? For a moment I wondered what she'd say if I did, if I told her the truth, whether she'd be angry, or would it just amuse her? If it did, I think that would have been worse.

But I didn't speak, I just thought once again how strange life was, that what you didn't want, you got, or rather, got it when you were least in need of it. I knew this wouldn't last, I couldn't make it last. Within a week, maybe even a couple of days, we'd be back where we always were, with me on my hind legs, begging her for scraps.

She said, in the dark, 'I'm destructive. Why don't you keep away from me?' I said, 'I can't. We were lying on our backs now, speaking into the dark, not seeing one another's faces. Things weren't real; we were almost talking to ourselves. She said, 'We interact, of course; that's the trouble.' I said, 'You know I can't follow all that stuff.' She said, 'Yes, you can. You don't want to. You hate people probing, don't you? You hate looking into yourself.' I said, 'We've been through this before. What good does it do?' She said, 'Why did you leave the stage? Have you asked yourself that?' I said, 'Have you?' She said, 'It was different with me, there wasn't any real sublimation. It was just a means of escaping from home.' I said, 'Perhaps it was the same with me.'

We were still in this No Man's Land, where whatever you said didn't count. Now she said, 'Nonsense, you were

64

very good, it really meant something to you. If you could find out why you blocked, it might be a great help.' I asked, 'To do what? To go back, again? It's far too bloody late.' She said, 'Not necessarily to go back; it might release you to do something else you could really plug in on, instead of all this advertising rubbish.' I said, 'Thank you,' but it hadn't really hurt; we were still in limbo. Besides, I knew that for once it wasn't meant to hurt. It still sounded like a lot of crap to me, though.

I said, 'It's a means to an end, that's all.' She said, 'But what end?' I said, 'Making a bloody living; something you don't have to do. You ought to be grateful.' She said, 'You feel guilty about it, that's why you're angry.' I said, 'Balls,' but I *was* angry, I wanted to justify myself, and before I could stop it, out it came, 'If you want to know, I'm writing a play.' She said, 'That's very good, why ever didn't you tell me?' I knew very well why I hadn't told her, I wished to God I hadn't, now; the play was rubbish, and I was terrified of her saying so. I said, 'Oh, it's not much good.' She asked, 'How much have you done?' and I lied, I said, 'I'm about halfway through.' She said, 'You're not blocked on that as well.' I didn't answer for a moment, then I said, 'Yes, since you ask.' She said, 'It's probably all the same thing.' I said, 'Is it? Well, you'll be relieved to hear that I am *not* blocked on my children's book,' and that note came into her voice, for the first time that night, that isn't-he-funny note, she said, 'Nor on your advertising?' I said, 'Sometimes, yes. Now tell me that's part of it, too.' She said, 'I shouldn't think so; advertising's something you don't want to do.' I said, 'And acting's something I *do* want to do, which is naturally why I gave it up. Thank you.' Then I turned my back on her, to go to sleep.

I heard her laugh, and in a few minutes, she slid her hand round the front of my thigh. I said, 'That's blocked, as well.' She said, 'Is it? Are you sure?' and went on playing with me, till I spun around and took her again, this time much more violently, hurting her and meaning to, biting and squeezing at her, till she came with a great, shuddering spasm.

She said, 'You hated me then, didn't you?' I didn't answer, and she gave another laugh, almost reflectively. She said, 'I must remember that; to make you hate me, again.'

Waking with her, there was no question of being given breakfast; she never had it, anyway, just a cup of coffee, and I was damned if I was going to make it for her, this morning.

She was still asleep. I got up and went into the bathroom, then hunted my clothes all over the sitting-room like some sort of paper chase. I felt down again; all that good feeling of the night before had drained away, all I could think of was her bloody probing, and on top of that, I had a hangover. For a moment, I thought of just slipping through the front door without a word, but then she called me from the bedroom, 'Geoff, what time is it?'

I said, 'Half past nine.' She said, 'Hell: I've got a hairdresser's appointment at ten; I'll have to ring and cancel it. Make me some coffee!' I thought, sod you, I nearly told her I'd an appointment myself, then I went into the kitchen and put some water on to boil. The kitchen was great, though she hardly ever cooked in it; all gleaming white, glossy white fridge and stove and dish washer.

When I brought her in the coffee she was sitting up, still naked, and the sight of her almost stopped me. If only she'd looked bad in the early morning, but she never did, she looked wonderful; having her hair all over the place only gave her that wild look. Her eyes were beautiful, and her breasts were so neatly shaped I wanted to reach out and take the nipple in my fingers. She must have guessed,

66

because she gave a grin and said, 'I only asked for coffee.'

It was a good moment to ask when could I see her again, and I started, but then the words wouldn't come out, I was afraid. She said, 'Bring me your play.' I said, 'All right. When?' It was a way through to her; I could always tell her I'd mislaid it. She said, 'Oh, I don't know. Ring me tomorrow.' I said, 'Okay,' and she said, 'Kiss me goodbye. Chastely.' I bent, and kissed her on the lips. As I got to the bedroom door, she called, 'Perhaps there's a part in it for *me*.'

Driving home, I thought how much I needed to get away, abroad; things were getting too real, I felt surrounded; Audrey, Jane, my mother. I needed some sunshine. What the hell was reality, anyway? Just being what other people wanted you to be. Audrey wanted me to take myself to pieces and see if I could put them together again, my mother wanted me to get married, and Jane wanted to marry me.

At a traffic light, looking at the windscreen wipers whirring on the glass, at the raindrops streaming down it like runners in a race, I suddenly thought of Rosemary, and felt better. *She* wasn't asking anything, except for what I wanted to give her. But she would; they always did. Besides, *I* wasn't the same, now that I'd passed this male menopause. I'd still got the physical energy all right, I'd proved that; it was the emotional steam that ran out of you. Maybe it was just that as you got older, you got more vulnerable, you started differentiating; it wasn't all just crumpet, any more. You reached Emotional Maturity, and there were times I thought that I could do without it.

Not long after I was back at the flat, looking at the whisky ads, John phoned. He said, 'Out on the tiles? I tried you twice.' I said, 'Just a hangover,' and he said, 'I see, you've been sleeping it off. Well, I'm glad I didn't wake you, or *have* I?' I said, 'No, you haven't.' He said,

'Good. Can you bear to talk about the book; to think of camels? You remember the one I mean.' I said, 'I think so.' He said, 'Good,' but I could tell he wasn't pleased. He said, 'I've done a few sketches I'd love you to see. That idea you had about a flying saucer.' My head was ghastly; I said, 'Can I ring you back?' He said, 'No, I'm going out, I'll ring *you*,' and hung up. I felt sorry, then I thought, oh, him as well; all of them ganging up, demanding, to hell with him, to hell with the bloody camel. And I suddenly had an idea, I laughed. We were in the Sahara, weren't we? Then why not a French nuclear explosion; goodbye, camel; the Sphinx's secret is safe.

I sat there looking at the whisky ads, and couldn't write a line. I needed to talk to somebody, but who the hell did I talk to? Jane? She was like a cascade of warm treacle; she told you whatever she thought you'd like to hear. Audrey? She was what she said she was, destructive; she didn't help you, she tore you apart, like she'd done to me, now. Rosemary? That wasn't a talking relationship. My mother, my father? That was a laugh. Funnily enough, one of the people I *could* usually talk to was John; about myself, that is, not about birds; then there were always undertones. He was someone who'd listen to you without an axe to grind; to *you*, not to some dummy they set up instead of you.

So the end of it was that I picked up the telephone and rang him back. He was prickly at first: 'Oh, yes?' I said, 'Look, I'm waking up, now. I'd like to see those things of yours, if you've got time. Why don't you drop in when you've been wherever you're going?' He said, 'I'll drop in *briefly* on the way,' which told me he hadn't been going anywhere, and he was round in half-an-hour, carrying a blue portfolio.

When I opened the door, he gave me his you-know-and-I-know smile. He had this way of implying that nothing ever meant what it said, but we'd pretend it did, because it made life easier. I suppose you'd call his whole attitude ironic, he used his irony as a sort of smoke screen, yet at the same time you felt that there was nothing at all vicious behind it; he might laugh at you, but he didn't want to crucify you.

He laid the drawings out on the table; they were pretty good, in the same, rather whimsical, way; little green Martians looking over the top of a flying saucer, and the camel looking back at them with a sort of snooty, quizzical camel look.

I said, 'They're very good. I don't know why you need me; the drawings stand up on their own.' He said, 'They're all your ideas.' I said, 'Yes, I suppose so. Some of them.' He said, 'Most of them.' I said, 'Yes. Jesus, I feel depressed.' He smiled again and asked, 'Audrey?' I said, 'Yes. She wants me to unblock.' He said, 'Come again?' and I said, 'To find out the reasons why I blocked on acting, and gave up.' He said, 'Don't you know them?' I said, 'Yes; I got pissed off with standing about in dole queues and sweeping people's floors. And with the idea of going out on a stage and spouting words and being someone else.' He said, 'Well, isn't all that good enough?' I said, 'For me, yes; not for her. She's looking for *motivations*.' He said, 'Oh, dear, I hope she *finds* them.' I said, 'Well, when she finds them, she can stuff them,' and his smile changed, I could see he liked that.

He said, 'One has to accept that people change. *I* once wanted to be another Henry Moore; I can't think why. All those draughty holes and that frightening austerity.' While he smiled, he was watching me, but I knew better than to join in the joke. I asked, 'Are you sorry?' He said, 'Sometimes. Are *you*?' I said, 'I'm sorry not to find anything else. Anything as big.' He looked at me for a moment, then he said, 'Well, we've found a camel.'

That night, I got out the play and read it through again. It didn't seem any funnier than it had, the last time; I could guess what Audrey would have said about it. I picked up the phone and rang her, but she wasn't there, and that sickened me even more. I needed a girl, I needed something; John had helped, but the thing was still there.

I couldn't phone Rosemary, her husband would be home, so in the end I rang Jane. I dialled her number twice and put down the phone, but the third time I let it ring, and she answered. She said, 'Hallo, Geoff,' she'd never dissimulate, she was always so bloody pleased. Sometimes it made me feel like kicking her, this time I found myself glad to hear it, I knew I'd done the right thing. She'd come round, she'd read the lousy play, she'd tell me for the hundredth time how great it was, then we'd go to bed and in the morning, she'd cook breakfast. Then I could put the play back in a drawer, and forget it again. I disgusted myself.

I said, 'I thought if you weren't doing anything, you could come over; I've got a few tins,' knowing the answer: 'Love to! I've got some steak in the fridge, I can bring that!'

She brought a present, too; a black leather tie, the kind I liked but knew she didn't. I said, 'Oh, Jane, for Heaven's sake!' and she said, 'It's funny you should ring, I only bought it this afternoon.' Like hell she did. Sometimes I thought she had a whole wardrobeful of things, very carefully chosen, all my style, and when she thought the time was right, she'd take one out: I just saw this, today. It would have been easier if I'd hated them, but I never did; she knew me inside out, that side of me; all they did was make me feel guilty. It would take weeks before the guilt wore off and they were just clothes, that I could wear and enjoy.

I didn't mention the play, I'd just left it where it was, strewn on the table, and sure enough she saw it, 'Oh, the play! Have you done any more?' I said, 'No, I haven't, actually. I was sort of revising.' She said, 'Geoff! Why don't you just finish it? You're such a perfectionist!' I shrugged. Perfectionist. She said, 'You are! You'll never get it done if you keep worrying what other people might think.'

I looked at her; she had the usual soppy expression on, soppier, because it was all plaintive; but she'd surprised me again, she'd understood me. Platitudes, platitudes, then right out of nothing, this. She looked back at me — you-know-how-much-I-care-about-you — and said, '*I* know how you feel. Why don't you let me take what you've done and show it to somebody? I could show it to our dramatic critic, and he knows thousands of producers.'

I said, 'Him? If a play isn't by Beckett or Pinter, he crucifies it.' She said, 'Please! Do let me!' and I nearly gave in, what harm would it do? If he did rip it apart, he wasn't telling me anything I didn't know. She said, 'You mustn't worry so much about criticism!' I said, 'All right, later on, when I've got a bit more done.' She was going to say something else, but I turned away from her, squared up the pages of typescript against the table, and stuck it away in a drawer.

She took it personally, of course; I might have been sticking *her* away. Her face fell like a child that's had its toy confiscated. I said, 'Cheer up: I'll finish it some day,' but she said, 'I'll cook the dinner,' and went out to the kitchen. Why don't you let me put it in the oven, and I'll bake it for you?

I poured myself a drink, I was on a vodka and tonic kick. I thought, with Jane I'm a playwriting dummy. This is Geoff: he's a playwright. Labelled. Terribly talented, never been performed. Just won't finish his play, or it would run for years. That's my mission; to make him. You see, these geniuses *need* a woman.

I wondered how she'd feel if I took the play out into the kitchen and said, 'Here you are, have it. You like it so much, you can finish it.' There'd be tears, obviously; why did I have to be so nasty, she was only trying to help me. She probably believed it, too; but she wasn't trying to help me, only the dummy.

In bed that night I asked her, 'Jane, why do you *bother* with me?' knowing what she'd say, feeling irritated before she'd even said it, 'Geoff, I love you.' I said, 'Honey, I'm a swine. I've told you again and again I make you unhappy.' She said, 'No, you're not. If you really were you'd never think so. Real swine never do.' There was logic for you; you couldn't win. She said, 'Besides, there's lots of times you make me very happy.' She deserved something for that. I took her hand and squeezed it; it was the least I could do.

There was a long pause, then she asked, 'Geoff: do I make *you* happy?' I said, 'Me? Yes, of course you do.' She said, 'Really happy?' Christ! I said, 'I'm very seldom really happy, doll.' 'Not even with me?' I made a big, big effort, I swallowed everything down hard, and I said, 'I said so, didn't I? Yes.' Now leave me alone and for God's sake go to sleep, before I say something I don't want to.

But that was enough for her, thank the Lord; after that, she slept, and I did, too. Before I dropped off, I remember wondering, did men and women always hate each other as much as they do now?

CHAPTER FOUR

I ran into Dave one afternoon, coming out of the Academy Cinema in Oxford Street. There'd been a Polish film I'd wanted to see; lots of heroics, men in sunglasses and leather jackets knocking people off like flies, with the Communists coming out the good guys. He didn't see me at first, he was looking round vaguely like an owl in the sun as if he'd lost somebody; or perhaps he was just shortsighted.

I said, 'Dave, isn't it?' and he focused on me then and said, 'Hi!' I asked, 'Enjoy the film?' and he said, 'Sure, he's got some great movement in that camera. You like it?' I said, 'Yes, when they weren't trying to push the message across,' and he laughed and said, 'That's part of the package. In Wardour Street, they ask you, is it commercial? In Warsaw, they ask, have you incorporated the party line, comrade?'

I asked him, 'Want a coffee?' and he said yes, quite eagerly. I got an impression I hadn't had before that he was lonely. We went to one of those Espresso places, with little dark sad men looking over the top of a great, shining, hissing machine as though they were its slaves for life. We talked some more about the film, then about other films, and I told him I'd like to work in the States. It's the sort of thing most Americans like to hear, and anyway it was true, but it seemed to worry him, like so many things did; this pain came over his face and he said, 'Stay here, don't try it. It's for people like Audrey; transients.' I didn't latch on, I said, 'She's been there a lot.' He said, 'Yes. This

73

time, she's staying six months,' and the room went dark, there'd been an earthquake, there was a huge hole underneath the table and I was falling, falling into it.

I said, 'Six months?' He said, 'That's what she says. *She'll* probably change her mind; you know Audrey. She'll get bored, then she'll take off for Acapulco or Bermuda and lie on another beach.'

I wanted to howl like a dog: she never told me! she never said a word! I wanted to ask him questions, when did she go, when did she decide? I had a dreadful feeling: that she'd gone the very day I made love to her, that this was *why* she'd slept with me.

When at last I could make sense again, I saw he was looking at me, quite sympathetically, not surprised at all; I wondered, had he guessed? I wondered, too, like I had before, was he her lover? He'd known; I hadn't. Or had he known just because he wasn't? That was possible; she was so very perverse like that. I said, 'Six months.' It was all I could manage; questions were a give-away. He said, 'Six months kidding herself she's getting something done, meeting people she gets tired of, looking at pictures she doesn't like, swinging so hard she thinks she's moving.'

For some reason, this made me feel a bit better. It was something I hadn't expected from him, and I wanted to hear her criticised; for what she'd done, what she was, the way she lived. I wanted someone else to say it was all wrong, that it was getting her nowhere. I said, 'I know what you mean. Running away from herself.' He frowned and said, 'Yeah, but we're all doing that. She hasn't even found out what she's running away from.' I said, '*She* thinks she has.' It came out very bitter. He said, 'Two years in analysis. She's picked up the patter. A little surface knowledge. It hasn't told her why she hates men. She maybe doesn't even know she does.'

I said, 'Hates men?' It was another straw. That explained it; she didn't just hate me, behave like this just to me. He said, 'She rationalises it in terms of what her father did to her or what her mother did—or didn't do. That's just another escape route.' I suddenly felt I could tell him. I said, 'As a matter of fact, I didn't know she'd gone,' and he smiled, he said, 'No?' I said, 'She plays some funny tricks.' He said, 'They're sadistic. She doesn't even play them on impulse; they're planned, she's an artist.' I was sure, then, he'd been involved with her, too, and almost sure there was nothing, now. There was a sort of retrospective tone to what he said; but then, there always was, as if he'd lived life out, and there was nothing left now but to commentate on it.

I asked him, 'Is she staying in New York?' He said, 'Yeah, with friends on Park and 65th, I think it is. Call me, I'll give you the address.' He'd got it, I hadn't.

When I left him, the good feeling went up in smoke. It was a cold, clear day with a bitter wind, early March, no rain, and the car was in dock; bloody steering trouble. I walked along Oxford Street with my coat open, not caring, while they came and came at me along the pavement in stupid hordes, the admass, the shopping crowds, sometimes bumping into me, but I didn't mind that, either. I was almost glad of it, I was glad to bump into them, the morons, with their glassy, senseless faces, more like zombies than people.

I felt sick. Not just upset: choked, revolted by what she'd done, by the feeling this was how she'd *meant* me to react. There was no real comfort for it, either; by telling myself she was sadistic, she was immature, she was really a mess, like Dave had said. It didn't do me any good, if anything, it only made it worse; it meant there was nothing to be done.

I wanted to go home and write to her, to tell her what a cunt she was, how if she'd meant to hurt me, she could feel bloody satisfied. Just *tell* her, just for *my* sake, just to get it

75

out. By the time I reached Park Lane, I'd written it three times. Somehow I got across the road, the mad motorway it was now, dodging the cars that came at you blind like the pedestrians, only worse, so much more dangerous; these were the morons with more money. And trapped in the middle of the road, between the double lanes, I had the feeling the whole world was bearing down on me; cars, people, everything, and soon they'd get me.

I walked home across the park, it was what I wanted, bashing along across the soggy green grass, under the skeleton trees, under a flat grey sky that gave you nothing.

Walking was better, the open air was better, I ought to have more of it, I knew that; I ought to eat less and drink less and take more exercise. I ought to give up the car and lose a stone. I'd been quite athletic at school, I'd played Rugby and thrown the discus and even done a bit of boxing — and now look at me. If I wasn't cooped up in my own flat or someone else's office, I was cooped up in that tiny car. It was unnatural; you forgot what grass was like and trees were like — even park grass, park trees — you forgot what it was like to be walking in the wind. And thinking about Audrey helped me along, it was like fuel, propelling me. I was belting across the park, and as long as I kept moving, I could live with it; it was there, but bearable, it wasn't destroying me.

Through Hyde Park, over the bridge across the Serpentine, into Kensington Gardens, still going like a bomb. Nobody much else out; a few dogs, a few prams and nannies. Out into Kensington High Street, down the Earls Court Road, up the stairs, into the flat, and there it was again, no escape, it had followed me all the way.

I got the vodka out and started drinking, there was nothing else for it, and vodka's a funny drink, insidious, it doesn't touch you at first, it slithers down, then suddenly bang! you're away, before you've even noticed it.

I got out some paper, I started writing to her, though I knew damn well I'd never send it. I wrote four letters, four different pages; how could you, how the hell could you? but by the fifth, the vodka was working, it was just abuse; you cunt, you cunt, you damned sadistic cunt. Then I screwed that into a ball, as well, and flopped out on the sofa; I was gone, it was what I'd wanted.

The phone went, but I didn't answer it. Jane: bound to be. She'd said, 'Shall I ring you tonight?' and I'd said, 'Okay; I may not be in,' but anyway, I was getting psychic about her phone calls. Crossing the park, I'd thought about asking her over and sleeping with her, but then I'd thought no, that was disgusting, using one as an antidote to the other, and besides, I knew I'd treat her badly, that when I wasn't having her she'd be annoying me, driving me up the wall; your play, your talent, what's the matter, darling? So I let it ring … and ring … and ring, knowing now it was her, no one else would ever have kept on like that, hoping that I might be there, maybe in the bathroom, or just about to come through the front door, or just not in a mood to answer, which might change, if the phone rang long enough. God, I'd done it myself, I knew.

At last it stopped, and I dropped off. I woke in the small hours with my head bursting apart, so bad that I couldn't think of anything else. I rolled off the sofa on to the floor, and lay there for a while, then I gradually hauled myself up, went into the bedroom, and fell on to the bed.

When I woke, the phone was going, it was morning, and my head was still murderous. I didn't take the phone. I got up, staggered into the bathroom, and swallowed four Codeine; then it started ringing again. I thought, bloody Jane, it's bound to be bloody Jane, but it wasn't, it was Cartwright, from the agency.

He said, 'Very disappointed with those whisky things.' I was groping, I said, 'Oh?' I thought, what whisky things, what's he talking about? He said, 'Good God, your copy, man, the copy you wrote for Dougall's Whisky!' I said, 'I'm sorry, I'm not quite awake.' He said, 'Well, it's eleven o'clock,' he sounded almost petulant, as if in some way I was meant to have let him down. I said, 'Well, I'm very sorry, I did my best with them.' It all seemed so trivial just now. He said, 'After some of your other work ... There's no originality here, nothing fresh. If the idea didn't do anything to you, why the hell didn't you come straight out with it and say so?' Because I needed the money, you nit. I said, 'I thought it might, at the time.' He said, 'Very well, you shall have your seventy-five guineas,' and hung up on me.

I thought, oh, screw him, and sat down on a chair, nursing my head, hoping the Codeines would work. *Do anything to you.* The stupid old sod; I was too angry even to feel upset, yet. What the hell *should* a whisky bottle do to you, except make you feel like having a drink out of it? *I* knew what he wanted, with his man-to-man crap and his colours of the regiment bit; he wanted to be reassured, he wanted people to tell him he was doing a gentleman's job that was worth doing, instead of dreaming up clever lies to take money out of people's pockets. Hanging up on me like that! I was so pissed off that I'd almost forgotten what was really wrong, and then it hit me, wallop; oh, far worse than the headache; Audrey; right in the pit of the stomach.

I crawled back into the bedroom and flopped across the bed, without the will to move. What was there to move for? I didn't sleep again. It was a strange feeling I had, complete apathy, a sort of paralysis. The pain ebbed away from my head, I noticed that vaguely, but it made no real difference. The phone rang quite a few times and I let it ring, what was there to talk about? It was like the pedestrians in Oxford Street, the cars; it was all coming at me. If I answered the phone or opened a letter, there'd only be more of it; I knew these cycles, if that was what they were. Once they'd begun, there was no fighting them. Cartwright wasn't going to give me any more work, that was obvious, not unless I rang him up and crawled to him or came up with another idea to pacify him, but I couldn't do that now, not with this paralysis. First came the earthquake, then the tidal wave, and the tidal wave swept everything along with it. If the big things went for you, you could deal with the little things, but when the big things went wrong, you couldn't deal with anything.

It was two o'clock when I rolled off the bed at last, and then it was to phone Rosemary. Not with any real hope; with women, you always had to be on top of the game, swinging, take it or leave it. They had radar; any hint of weakness, I-need-you, and it was, oh, it's you; not *this* week; can I ring you? Except for Jane, of course. Except Jane.

Still, you never knew, sometimes you could be lucky; like a car, sinking in the mud—it could never get out by itself, but maybe a breakdown truck would come along and haul it out. So I phoned Rosemary, and she answered it and said, 'Not now,' and put the phone down.

That did it, that was all I needed. I poured myself another glass of vodka; the bottle was nearly empty now, and all I had left was a quarter-bottle of whisky. When the phone went again, I waited till it stopped, then took the receiver off the hook and left it to buzz on the table. What I wanted was just amnesia, to step out of life for the next six months; except that I couldn't see any light even then. She'd be back, but what use was that? So I drank the vodka, and after the vodka the whisky, and the day dragged past and the afternoon post came through the letter box, and still I went on sitting there, drunk enough to kill the pain, so that Audrey was just floating there, somewhere out in space and not quite real, but anyway more real than the baby's face, the other nightmare, the one which would take over from it in time, because it stood for every other nightmare.

And then Jane came. God knows what time it was. The street door bell rang and I thought, to hell with whoever it was; it couldn't be anything good. Then it went again, and again, held for longer and longer, so I'd already guessed; then a knocking on *my* door, then her voice, 'Geoff!' as if she was frightened. I thought, damn her, the silly bitch, yet at the same time knew that I was glad, almost relieved.

I hauled myself out of the chair and blundered across the room, in the dark. At first I couldn't find the knob of the front door lock, then I managed to, and opened it, and there she was. She looked horrified when she saw me, saying, 'Geoff,' very high-pitched, and I mimicked her, 'Geoff!'

She came in like a district nurse, shutting the door, turning on the light, saying, 'Geoff, you look ghastly. What's the matter?'

I said, 'Nothing's the bloody matter.' I was half pissed. She said, 'When did you last eat?' I said, 'God knows. Yesterday.' Food: the answer to everything; there was nothing in the world that a good casserole couldn't cure.

We were in the living-room now; she snapped that light on, too, then looked at me and said, 'And when did you last get any *sleep*?' I didn't answer her, I sank back into the chair and closed my eyes. She said, 'I was worried about you, your phone was off the hook for *hours*, I couldn't think why.'

I thought, go away, go away, let me sleep, because I *could* sleep now, that was the funny thing; now that she was here. I didn't want her to leave, just to leave this room, or stay and be quiet. She said, 'I brought a roast chicken' —

I might have guessed — 'would you like some now?' but I shook my head; I couldn't even think of eating.

The other thing was, I hoped to God she wouldn't pester me, but she didn't, she didn't even seem upset about the chicken, in fact she was surprisingly calm. Looking back, I suppose the reason was she'd sized things up and knew she was winning, the way women do; that now she had to sit tight and play it cool. So it was, 'Why don't you go to bed? I'll bring you a hot drink.' I said, 'Yes, nurse.'

She found some cocoa somewhere, a tin she must have brought with her, or stuck in the cupboard some other time, perhaps anticipating this; I never drink the stuff, though now I was quite glad of it.

Christ knows how long I slept. When I woke, she was already up, standing by the bed; she said, 'I've brought you a cup of tea, and all these letters.' I said, 'You open them, don't read me the bad ones,' and she tore open a couple, one from John, where had I been — *that* got a pretty cold reading — the seventy-five guineas from Cartwright, thank God; no covering note — then a third, which she just put down, she said, 'You'd better read this when you feel stronger.' I said, 'Okay: give it me.' It was from the agency that had commissioned the butterscotch jingles; they didn't like them. I wasn't surprised; I hadn't liked them, either. In fact I somehow seemed to have accepted that I'd come to the end of the road, that there was nothing more I could do in advertising, though God only knew what I'd do instead. She said, 'The trouble is they don't want anything original, they just want the same old rubbish.' Loyal to the bloody last. I said, 'Mine weren't so original.'

I nearly told her, 'Anyway, I'm giving up advertising,' but I didn't need to, I knew already what she'd say, 'I'm so glad, Geoff, you're too good for it.' Hearing her say it would have annoyed me, knowing she'd say it was somehow comforting. She said, 'Will you be able to get your own lunch? I can come back from the office, if you like.' I said, 'Christ, I'm not an invalid.' She said, 'I'll cook you your dinner, then. What would you like?' and waited, I could read her face, is he going to say yes? Then I said, 'Okay,' very graciously, so she stayed that night as well; and the next night. And the night after that.

She wasn't just calmer out of bed; she was calmer in it. If I didn't want to make love, she just accepted it, we didn't get a big rejection scene, and when I did, she wasn't so completely dependent. There'd been times when she'd reminded me of a great big blob of wax, absolutely passive, taking whatever impression you made and being grateful. But now, she seemed to think she was protecting me. I was her child, poor Geoff, whom the world didn't appreciate, let me stroke you. It was in her expression, in her movements, even in the little sounds she made. I put up with it, though, just as I never said anything when after a time she stopped bothering to ask should she come round, could she stay? though *I* knew what was going on.

I suppose I must have had this need of her, but frankly, there was another thing as well, something I didn't like to think of much; I'd got no money. The seventy-five guineas helped, but I had an overdraft already, and I'd been relying on the rest of that, just as I'd relied on being asked to go on with the butterscotch crap. At a pinch I might have got a bit more work, I might have rung up Bill, he usually found something for me, but I knew there was no point; whatever they gave me, I was sure to make a balls of.

It was a funny sort of time. I didn't do much in the day, just wandered round the parks, which I enjoyed; sometimes to Hyde Park, sometimes to Kensington Gardens, often to Holland Park, the best of all, much more sheltered and intimate, with the stone walls and the formal gardens, the spiky, oriental trees still bright green in the middle of winter, and the peacocks, sulking in the cold. I'd sit on a bench among the flowerbeds, or near the lily pond with the fountain, and watch the au pair girls prancing by with their macs and pony tails and black stockings, like some sort of uniform. I didn't even try to pick them up.

The only work I did was with John; he relaxed me, too. Sometimes he'd come to me, but mostly I'd go to him; I didn't want a silent bristling match with Jane. He realised she'd moved in with me; I remember his expression that first time he came out of the bathroom, the smile, the eyebrows—after seeing her toilet things, marching across the basin shelf like a bloody army: shampoo, hairspray, perfume, talcum powder, deodorants.

One day, inevitably, Jane came across a few pages of our book, I'd left them lying on the table: 'Oh, that's the book you're doing with John. I love the *words*. I'm not quite so sure about the pictures, but that's something I don't know much about.'

It was a limbo time, I realised it even then, a sort of parenthesis at the end of which something was going to happen, though God only knew what. At the beginning I thought I was just waiting for Audrey, to settle things one way or the other, then I wasn't sure what it was, though I knew what Jane was waiting for. She was waiting for me to marry her, for time to drift by until I just accepted things, until I said, we might as well get married, rationalise it.

She was like the waves, nibbling away at a cliff, it was amusing to watch her. One day it would be, 'Darling, what shall I tell Marion?' 'Tell her what you like.' 'I mean about the flat, the month's coming to an end, she wants to know if I'm going to stay on or not. It seems silly, keeping on two places, and anyway, I can't really afford

83

to.' One between the ribs. 'Okay, then, tell her you're moving out.'

I knew Marion had done everything she could to stop her. Once or twice, I'd come in in the middle of what were obviously phone conversations Jane was having with her, I'd hear from the passage, 'But you don't really know him ... if you only understood him,' and quack-quack-quack from the other end; then, seeing me, she'd change the subject, or she'd chop it short. Marion was a bitch, but I didn't really blame her; she was right, I wasn't any good for Jane, I'd told her so myself, I'd probably agree with a lot of what Marion must tell her. I could imagine how it went; selfish, layabout, using you, philanderer; nothing I hadn't told myself, the nights I couldn't sleep. I wasn't faithful to her, either; I was still seeing Rosemary.

A week or so after Jane had moved in, I felt enough confidence to try her again, and this time, it was okay: 'Oh, you! I'm sorry about last time. Complications. I've got to be careful, at the moment.'

She came over the next afternoon, but before she did, I went around the flat, concealing evidence, and there was so bloody much of it, I hadn't realised how far Jane had taken over. Her make-up in the bathroom, her brushes and stockings and dressing-gown lying in the bedroom, her fashion magazines in the sitting-room, her red umbrella in the hall. Being married wouldn't have mattered; having another girl-friend, living with you: I knew that would have been the end of it.

When she came, she said, 'You seem nervous.' I said, 'Do I?' but I was, I was thinking, will she smell Jane's perfume? it's all over the sheets, all over the bloody bedroom; I should have sprayed the room, or something; wondering, should I make love to her in here? I sat down beside her on the sofa, I kissed her, then I slid my hand beneath her skirt. She said, 'I like that, let's go into the

84

bedroom,' and we did, I didn't take the cover off the bed, and it was all okay, if she noticed anything, she never said so. In fact as soon as I'd got her clothes off she was away, this desperation thing, again, writhing and gasping, coming every time. And I was drawn in, too, I forgot myself, there was nothing in the world but making love, till at last we were lying on our backs, her fingers stroking my cheek, and the room had turned almost dark. I suddenly thought Christ! She'll be back!

I must have started. She said, 'What's the matter?' I said, 'Nothing.' She said, 'You're so strange at times. You change, you seem to go away.' I said, 'I'm back again.' She said, 'Where did you go?' I said, 'Nowhere much. Just remembered I've got to go out to dinner.' She ran her leg over my thigh and she said, 'Somewhere nice?' I said, 'Not really. Boring.' She said, 'Somewhere where you'll find another frivolous married woman?' I said, 'It's a restaurant,' and she said, 'In that case, I'll allow it.'

She sat up, bent forward, kissed my cock, then swung her legs off the bed; she moved very gracefully. I heard her close the bathroom door, the water running, and I thought, oh, God, I hope she doesn't find anything, I hope she doesn't open the medicine cupboard. Because that was where I'd stuck them all, the pots and the tins and the bottles, behind tins and bottles of my own. And I had this vision of her coming in again, 'I didn't know you used Miss Dior.'

I looked at my watch; twenty past five, I knew Jane usually left her office at half past: sometimes earlier. I thought, Jesus, will I have to go through this, every time?

I got up and dressed, went into the sitting-room, and poured a whisky for me, a sherry for her; speed the parting guest. When she did go, I'd have to bring out all the bloody evidence again. I brought the drinks back to the bedroom just as she was coming out of the bathroom, still

85

naked, looking very fresh and slim and young, still wearing that nice smile. She said, 'Drinks, how gorgeous!' and I suddenly felt very fond of her. I bent forward and kissed her on the nipple, she said, 'Lovely!' and I wished for a moment it was her living here, no demands, no hurt feelings, no moaning. In the bedroom she said, 'Do you believe in monogamy?' She was standing in her slip, pulling her dress over her head; she did that elegantly, too. I said, 'I've never tried it.' She said, 'No, it's a silly question,' and pulled the dress on, blue wool, very nice, like everything she wore.

She said, 'You can't find everything in one person, can you? Why should people have to try?' and I was afraid she wanted to settle down to a cosy long discussion, tell me I'm not doing wrong. I tried to find the right note, I said, 'Monogamy's for monogamous people.' She said, 'Do they exist? *I* don't know. I suppose my husband's one.' I said, 'He's nuts about you, isn't he?' and she said, 'But that doesn't give him the right to control me.' She was reflecting on it; I could see there was more where that came from. I went over to her and kissed her, then I said, 'I'm nuts about you, too.' She said, 'Yes; and about all the others!' I said, 'There aren't any others,' and kissed her again.

When she'd gone, and I'd stood crossing my fingers that they didn't meet on the stairs, I started buzzing round the flat like a blue-arsed fly, pulling Jane's things out of the wardrobe, trying to remember where they'd been lying, putting her bottles back on the shelf in the bathroom, pulling the magazines from under the cushions in the sitting-room. Doing it, I suddenly felt as if I was acting in a French farce, darting here, darting there, listening for footsteps, keys in the lock. I'd have probably looked damned funny to anyone watching, but it didn't seem funny to me, which I suppose is what makes audiences laugh.

And she *was* home earlier than usual; I'd just put *Vogue* and *Harper's Bazaar* back on the table and sat down, thinking thank God, when there was the key. She said, 'Geoff, you look tired.' I said, 'I fell asleep.' She said, 'Poor thing, that's awful, in the afternoons,' which gave me a twinge. I said, 'Have *you* had a good day?' Husband, getting back from the bloody office. She said, 'Oh, not bad. Except that Vincent rang me.' I wondered was I meant to feel jealous, because I didn't feel anything, except sorry for him, poor nit.

She said, 'He's terribly upset. I think Marion must have told him I was living with you.' I said, 'I'm bloody sure she did.' She said, 'He was in quite a state. He kept saying that he had to see me.' I said, 'And?' She said, 'And I said no. What's the point? I'm living with you, I'm in love with you, I'm not in love with him,' and I thought how bloody practical women could be when the ball was in their court, how bloody ruthless.

She asked, 'Do you think I *should* see him?' Test. I said, 'Not if you don't want to.' She said, 'I think it's cruel to prolong things.' Very smug: got what I want, now, thank you. I wondered if Vincent would be phoning *me*—were my intentions honourable?—and what the hell would I tell him, if he did? No, of course they're not, I'm just exploiting her, but she likes it, so what's the odds?

In fact he didn't ring, he came round. It was one afternoon, the sun had been out, I'd just got back from Holland Park, when the bell went, and there he was. When he saw me, he looked as if he'd turn and run downstairs, he said, 'I'm terribly sorry to trouble you. You probably don't remember who I am.' I said, 'Yes, I do, come in,' and when he did, I offered him a drink. That seemed to embarrass him, I suppose he'd been working himself up for a big confrontation scene, and here I was being nice to him. He said, 'Yes ... no, thank you ... well, all right,' then he said, 'You can probably imagine why I'm here.' I said, 'I think so, yes.' He said, 'I don't want to be melodramatic but ... well, I happen to be in love with Jane.' I said, 'I know, she told me,' and he ducked his head, trying to get up steam again, and said, 'You see, I'm not sure that you're really good for her.' I said, 'I know I'm not, I've told her, but it never does any good,' and knew that he'd never believe I meant it.

He looked up at me, a really dirty look, then down again, and started playing with his fingers, but I didn't help him; it was his turn. At last he said, 'Well ... if you admit that.' I said, 'Well, what?' I was getting impatient with him. Didn't he know the score? Why should he expect to have things easier than the rest of us? He said, 'Well, if I was in your place ... ' I said, 'What would you do?' I could see how he irritated her. 'I suppose you'd be a gentleman, and step aside. What if I did? Are you sure it would make any difference?'

That seemed to deflate him completely, and I was sorry I'd said it. He mumbled, 'Yes, I see what you mean.' I said, 'Look, we've all been through this some time. It's a lousy world. You get what you don't want, and you don't want what you get. All of us.' He looked at me and said, 'Do you love her?' I said, 'That's got nothing to do with it.' He gave a sigh and said, 'No, I see what you mean. Perhaps it hasn't,' put down his glass, and got up. I wanted to tell him, 'Look, you can see her if you want to, it's all right with me,' but I stopped myself, he'd hate me for it, and if she found out, there might be trouble. I went to the door with him and said, 'If it's any consolation to you, I agree with you; you'd be better for her than I am.' He said, 'It's not much, is it?' and left.

CHAPTER FIVE

I started work again on the play. She'd hardly moved in when the campaign started, drip-drip-drip, how's your play coming on, darling? it's so good, you really should get on with it. Then the little barbs: I'd feel proud to be helping you; I think anyone who can help an artist is privileged. In other words, what am I paying the rent for? And it worked in the end; after a month or so, I lugged the damned thing out and stared at it all one morning; then in the afternoon I managed to write one page, and of course it was lovely, marvellous. After that it was always, 'What have you written today? Can I see it? Will you read it to me?' and it was always lovely, always marvellous, till after a while I thought, perhaps it's not so bad, and then, it can't hurt to finish it, at least it's something to do, and then, look at the tripe they're putting on, anyway, and then, perhaps it may even be good. I didn't really think it was, but these things have a sort of momentum; if you push hard enough and long enough they start rolling on their own and take you along with them.

I dreamed up an affair for the painter with one of those Kings Road dollies who spend their week in the Kenya Coffee House and their week-ends in Daddy's stately home; I'd known a few. In fact I got quite hung up on this part of it, showing up the whole phoney bit, and Jane went into hysterics every time I read some to her, 'Oh, Geoff, it's so funny.' *I* thought so, it was making me laugh when I read it, but I wanted to try it on somebody else, because

Jane hadn't got much sense of humour, bless her; in fact when she did laugh it was like something happening to her that she couldn't help. At the same time I was afraid of risking it, it only needed one person to read it and say it was crap, or to listen to me read it and not laugh, and that was it. Now and again Jane would say, '*Do* let me show it to Phil,' that was her drama critic, and I'd tell her, 'When it's finished, when it's finished.'

And all the while, she was having family trouble. It didn't take long to start; at the end of the very first week the phone went and a woman's snooty voice said, 'May I speak to Miss Jane Ridding? I understand she is staying there.' I said, 'She isn't in,' and she said, '*I* see; then will you kindly tell her to telephone her mother,' and put the phone down before I could say, 'Yes, ma'am, certainly, ma'am.'

When Jane did get in I said, 'Your mother phoned. She sounds like Lady Muck.' She blushed and said, 'There's no need to be nasty about her.' I said, 'I'm not, that's how she sounded,' then I imitated her, 'Will you *kai*ndly tell her to telephone her mother?' She said, 'That's her duchess voice, we always called it that,' and I said, 'Well, should I have scuttled back to the servants' hall?' She said, 'It's nothing to laugh about,' and I suddenly saw that she was in a state, almost in tears; this middle-class thing; girls, their parents, it was always so hard for me to plug in on.

She said, 'Oh, I *knew* it would happen; Marion must have told her. Now there'll be such a dreadful row.' I said, 'Well, tell them to get stuffed.' She said, 'I *can't*,' and I shrugged, I knew I wasn't being very sympathetic; I suppose, to be honest, what was at the bottom of it was a feeling that if they did make her leave me, it mightn't be such a bad thing.

She said, 'Geoff!' in a tone that I knew, a red-light tone. I said, 'What?' She said, 'You won't be angry with me, will you?' I said, 'Christ, Jane, out with it! How can I know until you tell me?' She said, 'I'll have to tell them that we're getting married, it's the only way to keep them quiet.' I said, 'Tell them what you like,' and picked up the evening paper she'd brought in.

She started to cry, then, and she said, 'You don't love me,' and I put the paper down, I said, 'For God's sake, Jane.' Because I *didn't* love her, I'd never bloody well told her that I did. She loved *me*—or that's what she told me—she'd moved in, she was living with me, she was meant to be happy about it, so what the hell did she want? But I went through all the motions, short of committing myself to what I didn't feel, patting her on the shoulder, kissing her, telling her, 'There, there!' getting her a drink. I said, 'You're twenty-six, honey, you're not dependent on them, you can live whatever life you want.' She sniffed and said, 'It's easier for you, you're a man.' She said, 'I wish you'd meet them,' so I met them.

We went over there for dinner, to their house in Chiswick, a very nice one, near the river, full of knobbly, okay pieces of old furniture and corny paintings and cosy cushions. Her father reminded me a bit of Cartwright, not physically—he was smaller and heavier and squarer—but in his manner; the same staccato officer-and-gentleman stuff (I'd obviously been promoted from the ranks), except with him, it didn't seem to be quite such an act. Jane had said, 'His bark's worse than his bite,' which was probably true; in fact it seemed to me that he barked on sufferance, that it was Mrs Ridding who had her hand on the leash. He was about five foot nine, with a pallid face, grey hair parted down the middle, and big grey eyes that always had a look of surprise. She was a biggish, Boadicea sort of woman, black-haired with a hefty bust and thick legs, spectacles, a mouth and nose like Jane's, but none of that softness in the eyes.

He was a stockbroker; we lived on different planets, I'd

known we must, and the one thing I wasn't going to have was a heart-to-heart, a what-about-my-daughter? I'd told Jane that before I agreed to go. Looking at him, listening to him, I could imagine how it would go, how bloody futile it would be: 'Can't have her compromised, you know,' plus all the bullets his wife would have made for him to fire.

But she liked me, I could tell that quickly, perhaps before she knew it herself. She kept switching points like a signal box, one moment smiling, responding, the next remembering that I really wasn't suitable. I saw her exchange a look with him now and then, usually when I said something — my accent, I suppose — and once or twice they tried to pump me. 'I understand you're a *writer*, Mr Barnes,' that was her, 'but that you used to be an *actor*.' 'That's right.' 'But aren't the two very different?' 'He's writing a play, Mummy.' '*I* see. And will the play be put on?' 'I hope so.' 'It's terribly good, Mummy.' 'I'm sure it is, darling, but there do seem to be so many.' Cow. 'Not one of those kitchen sink things, is it?' Him. 'No.' 'It's a comedy, Daddy.' 'Well, that's a pleasant change. Haven't seen a decent comedy for donkey's years.'

I thought of our heart-to-heart again: 'As a matter of fact, sir, your daughter's keeping me while I write it.' He'd probably have had a stroke.

'What else are you writing?' 'I'm writing a children's book.' 'Do those go well? Excuse my being so inquisitive; I don't know much about writing.' You could see that from the books on the shelves: encyclopedias, Foyle's Book Club, Georgette Heyer.

At the end of the day she said, 'Well, you must invite us to see *you*,' and I rather admired the old girl for that, it must have needed quite a deep breath. I said, 'Yes, of course,' and Jane said, 'Lovely, Mummy.' She was so pleased, it was pathetic.

Driving back she said, 'I think Mummy took to you.' I said, 'Yes.' She said, 'Darling, what's wrong?' I said, 'Nothing.' I was thinking what a fiasco it was, the post mortems that must be going on, about me: was I good for her, did I make a living; the talks there'd be with Jane: was she *sure* about me? and all the time there was nothing in it. But what was the use of telling her that?

She asked me, 'Didn't you like *them*?' Go on; hurt me. I said, 'Yes, they were fine.' She said, 'You didn't, did you?' I said, '*Yes*, for God's sake, *yes*! I'd tell you if I hadn't.'

The rest of the way back, we didn't talk; she was in tears, but I felt too choked to do anything about it. In fact neither of us said a word till we were in bed with the light out, then she asked me, 'Geoff: are you angry with me?' I said, 'Not with you.' She said, 'Why are you angry at all? Because of Mummy and Daddy? I know they're old-fashioned and snobbish ... ' I said, 'Oh, I expected to be disapproved of.' She said, 'Darling! You know what I meant.' I said, 'Look: you wanted me to go; I went. I've made the gesture, I've been through the motions. They've seen me. I've got two legs and two arms. I don't quite speak the Queen's English, and I'm not making any money. Okay, so now they know.' She said, 'You're beastly,' and she lay there crying till I weakened and gave in and made love to her.

It was odd, living with a woman again. I'd done it before, several times; I'd even lived with Audrey for a month in Littlehampton, my last month in rep, but by and large I'd got used to living alone, and it wasn't easy to readjust. It wasn't so bad in the week, I had the flat to myself all day, but at the week-ends it was too small, there was no escaping one another. The worst thing of all was what I called her reverent hush — he's working. I'd sit at the table with the play in front of me, or what she thought was the play, and she'd tiptoe round the room, *I* won't disturb him—she might as well have marched round it with a fife-and-drum band.

In any case, I liked being alone—when it was by choice. If you felt tired or depressed, you didn't have to say yes darling, no darling, answer silly questions, smile when it killed you, otherwise 'You don't love me.' And women take over, which means they re-arrange things, put things where *they* think they ought to go, and you can never find them, give the place 'a woman's touch', when you don't want a bloody woman's touch. In a way it's like a fifth column, undermining you from within. The bathroom goes first, that's where a woman lives, with all her sprays and bottles and douches, then the bedroom falls; *her* things everywhere—she always has more clothes than you —and little by little, the rest of the place. 'Darling, I've seen this; darling, I've just bought that.'

John came round one day and said, 'It's changing.' I said, 'I know.' He said, 'Much comfier, of course, but much less you,' and I looked at him quickly, but his face was a blank.

We'd nearly finished the book, now; he'd shown the publisher most of what we'd done, and apparently he was high on it, he wanted us to do another, and the agent thought he might sell it to America. I'd thought, great, I'm on fifty per cent, all I have to do is write ten of them a year and I can make a living.

They were still a bit cat and dog, John and Jane, circling one another, armed neutrality, each of them getting used to the idea of the other, because they had to. I think she was a bit afraid of him, his hints, his undertones, but after all, she'd won now, from her point of view, she'd moved in, and now she could let herself be gracious, couldn't she?

One evening he asked us both round—his first big gesture—and it didn't go too badly, really. He played some records she liked, showed her his art books, and had a couple of other friends there, a composer and his wife, 'interesting people'. He had black hair growing low down his forehead, the sort of man who looks as if he's been born wearing glasses, with one of those clever, nervous smiles. I wondered afterwards if John had chosen them with ulterior motives, he had plenty of them, because in a way they were a parody of Jane and me, she 'cared' about his music. He sat and smiled, all deprecating, while she did a P.R.O. job for him, the symphonies he'd written, the chorale that was going to be performed, the B.B.C. this and the Festival Hall that.

'Marvellous.' (Jane: very flat, I wanted to piss myself.)

'As a matter of fact, John's got a record of it.'

Cue for a song.

'I'll put it on.' (Cue taken.)

'Oh, no; not now.' (Still modest.)

'Come on, let's hear it.' (Me, for God's sake.) And it served me right, jangle jangle, miles above my head, not a note you could respond to, on and on for half-an-hour, and I imagined them up there on the platform, pouring water out of one bucket into another, twanging the strings, and doing all the other things they do now, when they're really with it: it seemed to be missing *something*. He sat through it as if he was ashamed of it, she had her eyes closed with her hands over her face, she could have been overwhelmed or just embarrassed, John wore his Mona Lisa look, Jane and I tried to keep awake.

It was hardly over when she said, 'Geoff's working on a play.' I could have kicked her. 'Oh, really?' How madly boring.

So it turned into a one-up match between her and this woman, except that Jane hadn't any shots to fire, and had to fall back on the past: 'He was on the stage, you know.'

'Oh, Christ, that was years ago; I've nearly forgotten.'

'Ben's writing for the cinema.' Beat that. And John

95

sitting there with his bloody smile, missing nothing, loving it. Still, at least it wasn't *him* Jane was fighting with.

When we got home she said, 'That woman made me furious. On and on about his music, his concertos.' I said, 'Well, you can't really blame her, if she's got something to talk about.' She said, '*I* didn't think much of his music, all those horrible discords.' I said, 'You may not like it, I may not like it, but it's been performed.' She said, 'What if it has?' I said, '*It* has, my play hasn't and I just wish you'd stop promoting me as if it had.' She said, 'I'm proud of you.' I said, 'Yes, that's sweet, that's very nice, but you might wait until there's something to be proud of. At the moment there's nothing.' She said, 'Well, *I* think there is,' and I shrugged.

She gripped my arm and said, 'You don't believe in yourself, that's the whole trouble.' I said, 'For Christ's sake, I know what I can do and what I can't. I could act a bit once, and that's about the size of it.' She said, '*And* you can write, darling.' I said, 'Sure; I'll be another Enid Blyton,' and her face fell; it was really a funny thing, she took all this much harder than I did; jabbing at her was like jabbing at part of myself, a part that sickened me, and perhaps that's why I did it.

We had our social life, now; she saw to that, suitable couples, most of them a bloody pain in the neck. I'd never had a social life before and I'd never wanted one, unless you counted the Markham and the Kenya in the Kings Road or Finch's in the Fulham Road when I was making the scene in Chelsea. I knew what she was up to, again, it was the married bit, nice young married people; look at them, dear, how happy they are. I'd no idea whether they were happy and I didn't care, to me they just seemed wet.

Some of them weren't quite so bad, there was a little red-haired man, shy and fairly funny, who worked on the book page of her paper, and his wife; plain and mousy. I noticed most of them were plain; this seemed to be a condition.

Then there was her elder brother — another one was in Canada, thank God — a great big Rugger hearty who frigged around in Lloyd's, friendly in a sort of shaggy-dog way, but a terrible drag. 'The theatre, eh? I suppose it's a pretty precarious sort of life, isn't it?' He came from his father's planet. His wife was tiny, pale and blonde, she might have been quite attractive if she ever woke up to the fact she was alive. 'Did you like them, Geoff?' 'Yes, loved them.'

Still, there was Rosemary. I brought her to the flat a couple more times, once in the morning, once early in the afternoon, but the grand transformation scene was getting too much for me; besides, she wasn't stupid, she was bound to notice sooner or later how the flat was changing, she may have noticed already; I'd caught her looking at me once or twice with a sort of smile.

She'd got to the let's-go-to-places-together stage; let's go and see that exhibition, let's go and see that film — look at all my *other* interests — which was a waste of good time in bed; besides, there was always a chance you might be seen.

I asked her, 'How about *your* flat?' but she wasn't keen. She said, 'What's wrong with yours? It's so much safer.' I said, 'I don't know. Just for a change.' She said, 'You're not one of those depraved types who want to make love to me on my husband's bed?' I said, 'How did you guess?' and in the end she gave in, she said, 'Just once,' and I went round there one afternoon, while the kids were still at school.

It was the sort of flat I'd expected, careful-contemporary, her not him, trying to be with it and not quite making it, pale colours and spiky Scandinavian furniture, a Cézanne reproduction over the electric fire in the drawing-room. What did surprise me was her own paintings, they really weren't bad, in a conventional kind of way; there were several of them hanging on the walls, mostly landscapes,

97

parks, little seaside villages. I said, 'They're terrific. Honestly,' and she laughed and said, 'Don't sound so astonished!' I said, 'I'm not,' and she said, 'I know what you think of me.'

The bedroom had a nice, big, low, square double bed and I noticed she'd taken off the counterpane. I said, 'Yes, I like this room.' She smiled and said, 'You *are* a swine,' then I put my arm round her and kissed her.

We made love on top of the bed, not in it, but otherwise she was the same as ever, nothing held back, no looking over her shoulder. I said, 'It's better here,' I meant it, though I admit I had an ulterior motive, saying so. She laughed and said, 'Why?' but of course I couldn't tell her. She said, 'I was right, you *are* perverted.' I said, 'Me? Look at me?' I had an erection, and so we made love again.

In the middle of it the phone rang by the bed, it rang and rang and rang, till you couldn't shut it out, it beat in your head, it even began to set the rhythm we were making love to. She hissed at me, 'Quickly, quickly!' and I went faster, till at last she drew in her breath, her body went rigid, and she came; and still the phone kept ringing. I pulled out and rolled over, to lie beside her; her eyes were shut, she said, 'Oh, God!' and stretched out a hand for the receiver.

Her husband's voice said, 'Rosemary? Where were you?' She said, 'I was asleep,' and yawned, very clever. He said, 'Asleep?' as if he didn't believe it. She said, 'Yes, darling. You know I had an awful night.' He said, 'Yes.' Obviously he didn't. 'Well, I'm sorry. I just wanted to tell you I got those tickets for Covent Garden.' She said, 'Marvellous!' and reached out and touched my cock. He said, 'Middle of the third row, stalls,' and she said, 'Marvellous,' still with my cock in her hand, then, when she'd put the phone down, she took it off again at once. She said, 'Oh, God, aren't I a bitch?'

CHAPTER SIX

———◆◆◆◆◆———

I rang Dave one day and we met for a drink. He drank tomato juice; in a big hand like his, it looked ridiculous. We met in Campden Hill in the Windsor Castle; I liked the pub but never liked the people, the chinless idiots talking about their cars — 'Don't think I know him; what does he *drive*?' — but it was halfway from where we both were.

He said, 'Audrey? She's in Mexico City. I knew she'd wind up in Mexico. I had a postcard,' and it hit me, though I'd thought I was over that, at least for the moment. He said, 'Next stop Acapulco, if she hasn't been there already,' and I said, 'I know, you told me. What did she say?' I tried to make it casual, I couldn't ask, when is she back? He said, 'Oh, nothing, just the normal postcard jazz, sun's shining, having a great time'; and that stung me, too. A great time.

I said, 'And she's away six months … ' He said, '*She* doesn't know. It depends who she meets,' then realised he'd dropped a clanger and said quickly, 'How's advertising these days?' I said, 'I've given it up.' He looked at me as if he found that very intriguing and asked, 'For what?' I said, 'Oh, nothing special. I'm writing a bit.' He asked, 'What kind of thing?' I said, 'A play, a book for children,' and he laughed and said, 'You sound like me; the artist type.' I said, 'What's that?' He said, 'A phrase Thomas Mann invented, a guy with an artist's temperament but no specific talent.' I said, 'That's me all right,' I was

99

choked, 'that's me, lazy and untalented.' He said, 'No, no,' laughing, 'that isn't what it means; not *un*talented, no *specific* talent, and every artist's lazy; only they call it blocked.'

But I knew well enough what it meant. I thought about it after I'd left him; it meant having the worst of two bloody worlds, too off-beat to fit into the square, conventional one, not gifted enough to achieve anything outside it.

That night, when Jane brought up the subject of the play, I snarled at her, because I'd had a nasty feeling. She was an angler, I was the stupid fish, the play was the worm on the hook, and I'd swallowed the hook and swum off, she'd let me swim for miles, then one day, in her own good time, she'd reel me in. There I'd be, one artist type, hooked, gaffed and landed, ready for dehydration. I felt like telling her, '*Your* play, you mean; the one you're using for your own bloody ends,' but what was the point? It might be true, and she might not even know it. The artist type. Oh, yes, it fitted.

In bed that night I had a terrific temptation to tell *her* and ask, 'Do *you* see me like that?' knowing what would come, the '*No*, Geoffs,' despising myself because I needed them. Because it was so damn true; just look at me, my acting, a quick flash in the pan when I was very young, then nothing, no staying power; I'd never had that and that was part of it, part of a real talent. So here I was, nothing; neither fish nor fowl, envying the real artists, because they'd got it, even envying the squares, because at least they were happy in their Philistinism, they never knew what they were missing.

On the first Sunday of the next month, I took Jane over to Harringay—and they liked her. I wasn't really surprised; what was there to dislike? She was sweet, she was kind, she was pretty, she was generous. I knew all these things, I could appreciate them, objectively, it was only subjectively that at times she nearly drove me up the wall.

My father went for her obviously, the moment he saw her, I could tell from the look on his face; seaside picture postcard; haw-haw, what have we here? then going very gay, winks and nudges, corny jokes — 'Have a sherry — if your mother lets you drink' — not his usual style, at all. And she did very well, laughed when she thought she was meant to, helped Mother in the kitchen, dried the dishes, talked to her about cooking and the price of vegetables; it was a swinging performance.

My mother said, 'Well, I like her, Geoff.' I said, 'Yes, she's very nice,' and she gave me a dig in the ribs and said, 'She's very fond of *you*.' I said, 'Yes, I know.'

My father said, 'This one's more like it. Why don't you bring her again?' I said, 'Yes, I can see you like her!' He said, 'Come off it, I'm too old for it. Known her long?' I said, 'I'm living with her.' It would have to come out some time. He pursed his lips and gave a whistle; he said, 'Don't tell your mother,' and I wondered whether *she* had. He said, 'Think you'll marry her?' throwaway stuff, he was never quite sure how to come at me, I knew, and it made me feel sorry for him. In fact I suddenly thought of Jane's father, both of them, hers and mine, advancing behind an act, mine all Rotary Club patter, hers with the plain, blunt City man bit. I said, '*She'd* like to,' and he said, 'You could do a lot worse. Have you met her family at all?' I said, 'Yes,' which was all I wanted to say, but he asked me, 'What's her father do, then?' I said, 'Stockbroker,' and he said, 'That can be very useful, with the tips they get.' I looked at him and he was dead serious.

Later on my brother and his stupid wife came round, and Jane talked to *them*, too, she could get down to their dreary level, when I couldn't even be bothered to try; I sat in an armchair and just cut off, picking up the odd phrase; about holidays and bottle feeding and what had been on telly. Now and again I'd see Dad and my brother looking at Jane, little, furtive glances. I didn't blame them, though I knew my brother must be hating me again; I had all the luck. Luck. But when my mother looked at her, she beamed, I couldn't remember seeing her so happy, and I knew why she liked Jane, why they'd both taken to her (apart from his fancying her). She didn't frighten them. Now and then I'd brought other girls down, girls I was more or less thinking I might marry, and they'd gone on their guard. They'd met Audrey once when they'd come down to Littlehampton, and she'd petrified them; mother had barely said a word, though he'd been attracted, of course. But when he did look at her, it was almost with a scared look, I could understand it, he'd never met anything like her.

When Jane and I left it was, 'Lovely ... *nice* to meet you ... see he brings you again soon ... don't wait till next month.' In the car, driving back, she said, 'Do you think they liked me, Geoff?' and I didn't answer for a minute. What was she up to? What the hell did it matter if they did? She said, 'Did they, Geoff?' and I said, 'You've got eyes, haven't you?' She said, 'There's no need to be horrible.' I said, 'Christ, they loved you, they adored you, they ate you up, you charmed the arse off them, okay?' She said, 'You have to spoil everything.' I said, 'Go and see them; you don't need me. Any time you like, they'll be delighted to see you. Charm them again,' and then the tears came, sniff ... sniff ... sniff, until at Marble Arch I said, 'Okay, okay, I'm sorry.' She blew her nose and said, 'You love upsetting me.' I said, 'No, I don't, honey, I feel terrible.' She said, 'Why do you do it?' but I just squeezed her hand. Where did you start?

CHAPTER SEVEN

One day, Rosemary said, 'Who is she?' She was lying beside me on my bed, with a sunbeam playing straight across her body, gold on white.

My stomach flipped and I said, 'Who's who?' and she laughed and said, 'Oh, come on, Geoff, I've known for ages. The girl you're living with.' I didn't look at her, I said, 'A girl called Jane.' She asked, 'Nice?' just a little too casually. I said, 'All right. She wants to marry me.' 'And you?' I said, 'I don't. If you really want to know, she's been paying the rent.' Jesus, I loathed myself. She said, 'Living on women. You're an even bigger cad than I thought.' I said, 'I don't know what I am.' I turned away from her and lay there on my side, wishing I was dead. But it actually seemed to amuse her, she ran her fingernail down my back and said, 'You're not going to sulk, are you?' I said, 'No,' and didn't move, because this bitterness was coming up inside me — bloody women — against her, against Jane, against the lot of them, however unfair it was. I resented her finding out, I resented Jane even more because there was something to *find* out; I thought, Christ, why must life be so complicated?

Behind me, she said, 'Cheer up!' She'd obviously forgiven me, you never bloody knew with women; no logic, no consistency, treat them like shit and there they were, adoring you. It sickened me. She said, 'The times you weren't here and she answered the phone; all those bottles in the bathroom: and today you forgot to hide her hairbrush.'

I said, 'Very funny,' and swung off the bed; I needed a moment by myself. I went into the bathroom for a pee, and there was the hairbrush sure enough, right on top of the lavatory cistern, with Jane's hairs in it. Beside it was a lipsticked cigarette end, Rosemary's, and I wondered if this was a joke of hers; I threw it into the bowl and flushed it away. I hadn't got her number, and she worried me; I was afraid of losing her, of being thrown right back on Jane; she reconciled me to Jane.

I came back into the bedroom and I said, 'Look, if you really want to know ... ' but she stretched out her arms and said, 'Make love to me; then you can tell me.' So I made love to her, I felt really fond of her, grateful, thinking that I hadn't lost her, and afterwards, with my face buried in her hair, breathing the scent of it, not seeing her, I said, 'I don't love her, if that's what you want to know.'

She said, 'Poor girl, you don't love her, you're living on her ... ' I said, 'That's temporary.' She said, 'I'm sure it is,' and then, 'Does *she* know you don't love her?' I said, 'Yes. Or if she doesn't, she should. I've never told her I do.' She said, 'Sure?' I said, 'Sure,' and she said, 'And yet you're living with her.' I wanted to explain, but I couldn't, there were things I only half understood myself, and that half I couldn't put into words.

She said, 'Is she pretty?' and she didn't sound jealous. I said, 'Not bad. Yes, I suppose she is.' She said, 'Dark or fair?' she was enjoying this. 'Dark. About as tall as you.' 'Good figure?' 'Yes.' 'She sounds as though you *ought* to marry her. I could never be as faithful as she is.' I said, 'Faithful. Oh, yes, she's faithful,' and she said, 'That's very *nice*.' I said, 'She's as faithful as a steel trap,' and Rosemary said, 'Now you're being nasty,' and I realised how she felt, she felt she'd won, it gave her a kick, like deceiving her husband. 'Poor girl,' she was giving her a pitying pat, and I felt bad, I didn't want to be included in the conspiracy. I said, 'I've told her I'm a swine, she ought to know, by now.' She pushed her finger into my navel and said, 'No, you're not. Just a man; no better or worse than the others.'

When she'd dressed, she asked me, 'Have you got a photo of her?' I said, 'No.' She said, '*Aren't* you hard? Not a grain of sentiment!'

After she'd gone, I went through the usual rigmarole of putting things back where they belonged, thinking that at least there'd be no more of *that*. I felt depressed as hell, I wanted to jump clean out of myself. It could never be the same, now she'd found out, or rather, now I knew she'd found out; the funny thing was that I could see now it mattered more to me than to her.

I picked up the telephone and rang John, asking could I come over and work, then I left a note for Jane. I couldn't face her.

When I got back she was upset; she still had this same thing about John. She said, 'You might have *told* me; I was going to cook such a super dinner,' and I said, 'I couldn't help it, something came up; we had to get on with some revisions.' Which was partly true, though in fact it had come up days ago and I'd just left it; we needed to make changes for the American edition. Because the funny thing was that the damn book was taking on a life of its own, the Americans loved it, they were going to pay a thousand dollars advance, and now we were planning another one, *Algy The Affectionate Alligator*. When I'd told Jane about it, I'd been quite excited, and she'd said, 'Oh, Geoff, that's marvellous,' as if it was a line she'd learned and didn't believe in. She said, '*I* see,' in a flat little voice, and I got irritated, I said, 'Don't ask how it's going!' She said, 'But I thought you'd finished it, darling!' and I said, 'Not the American edition, which *happens* to be bringing in some money.' She said, 'You *know* I'm glad; you *know*

I'm interested in everything you do.' I said, 'Oh, yes. Especially the play.' She said, 'Why *not* the play? Children's books are fine, but there's much more of *you* in the play.' I said, 'Yes, that's exactly why it'll never get put on,' and she got upset, as if she was defending me against someone else, she said, 'You're always running yourself down. You're always underrating yourself.' I said, 'Well, you're always overrating me, so it evens out, doesn't it? Wait till I've finished the play, if you don't believe me. Wait till you start showing it to people, because *I* won't. Wait till your little critic friend has read it.'

She looked completely dejected and said, 'I don't know why you resent me so much, just for wanting to help you.' I said, 'I don't resent you. If there's anything I resent, it's me, because I'm phoney, I haven't *got* it, I'm just indulging both of us by writing this thing.' She said, 'You're not, you're not!' and now she was crying. I said, 'You've got to accept it, *I've* got to accept it. But children's books may be something I can do. Children's books may be something in my range; they're probably about my mark,' and she cried, she said, 'First Mummy, then you.'

I sighed, I said, 'What about Mummy?' She said, 'She phoned when you were out, I had her on the telephone for an hour. First she said they were both very upset we still hadn't asked them over, then she got on to how worried Daddy was about me, when were we planning to get married, was I really sure about you?' I said, 'Well, why didn't you *tell* her?' I was bloody exasperated. I said, 'Why weren't you honest with her, why didn't you have the guts? Why didn't you say, "We're not *getting* married, we may never be getting married, and I'm a grown-up girl and it's my bloody life, not yours"?' which started an absolute bloody Niagara: I didn't know, I'd never understand.

I said, 'All right, I *don't* understand, but just don't drag me into it.' I thought, Christ, you'll be asking for a bloody ring, next; but I didn't say it. I told her, 'Look, they've got to find out sooner or later. If you're afraid to tell them, I will.' She said, 'No, no!' in a panic, and I saw what it was she was up to, she was clinging on; if she admitted it to them, she admitted it to herself, but if she clung on long enough, perhaps I'd change my mind.

I sat down beside her, put my arm round her, and said, 'Honey, let's not kid ourselves.' She said, 'I'm not! She went on and on at me. She'll never leave me alone, now.' I said, 'Well, what do you want me to do? Come on? What do you want me to *do*?' but she just kept crying. I stood up and said, 'Okay, have her over, if you think that'll do any good. Have her over, and we'll go through the pantomime.' I walked out of the room and slammed the door, but where was there to go after that? Only the bathroom or the bedroom.

So her mother came: on her own, one evening, for 'coffee'. She came in like the prow of a ship, it was a great entrance, 'And how many rooms *are* there?' 'There's a bedroom, a bathroom and a kitchen, Mummy,' looking round the living-room as if she could smell dry rot, saying, 'Very nice,' in a voice like an icicle, 'may I see the rest of it?'

I said, 'Yes, we'll take you on a conducted tour,' so she had a good, hard, dirty look at the bedroom, a quicker one at the kitchen ('It's a super cooker, Mummy') and an even quicker one at the bathroom ('We're going to redecorate soon, Mummy.' Were we?) Back in the living-room, you could tell I'd failed the test just by the way she sat down — very slow, absolutely breathing disapproval — but then I'd never asked to take it. She sat there, now, like a dowager, graciously accepting things, coffee, biscuits, compliments ('Don't you look well, Mummy?') while I sat there feeling more and more non-U, which I suppose I was meant to.

In fact after a time I just shut up altogether, I left them to it, and the conversation kept grinding down, with Jane trying desperately to start it up again; a dress she was thinking of buying, had they heard from her brother in Canada, how was Daddy's rheumatism or arteriosclerosis or whatever the hell it was, turning to me now and then and asking, 'Don't you think so, Geoff?' 'Yes.' Or, 'Wasn't that what *we* thought, darling?' 'Was it?' till Mummy went into second gear and began to come the gracious lady, drawing out the peasants, did I under*stand* cars? They'd had *so* much trouble with their Bentley. I said, 'No, I'm afraid my family runs to builders, not mechanics,' and Jane leaped in, 'Geoff's hopelessly unmechanical, Mummy.'

Mummy sort of rolled with the punch and came right back again, she was quite a game old bird, 'Your play that Jane keeps speaking about; how's *that* getting on?' I said, 'Lousy.' 'Oh, darling, it isn't; it's marvellous, you'd love it, Mummy, you ought to read it.' 'I should be very interested.' 'Do get it, Geoff, do read some of it, *please!*' 'I've no idea where it is, I'm afraid.' I knew she was going to say, '*I* have!' and jump up like a bird dog, but then she caught my look. Her mother said, 'I shall have to wait till it's performed, then. You must invite me to the first night.' I said, 'All right; if there ever is one.'

Jane had gone quiet, now, she seemed to have given up at last; when I looked at her face, it was pale and miserable, and for a moment, I felt sorry for her. But it was too late; once I was on this sort of kick, I couldn't stop, it was like going down a helter skelter. When I pitched at the bottom, I'd regret it, but until I did, that was it. *I* didn't speak, either, so there we sat, three waxworks, Mrs Ridding with her coffee cup halfway to her mouth, frozen, as if she'd forgotten it was there.

She had to take over. I wouldn't, Jane couldn't, so she did. She tried the weather and the Royal Family and the Government and how rude people were in the shops, and she got some vague answers from Jane, but only grunts from me; I still hadn't reached the bottom of the helter skelter. So she went; there was nothing else to do, looking at her watch — 'It's terribly late, darling.' 'Oh, Mummy, *do* stay!' 'No, dear, your father will be waiting up for me.'

So we saw her downstairs, into her Zodiac — the second car, the one that wasn't giving trouble — 'Thank you *so* much for having me, it was nice to see you again, Geoff' — and off she went.

When the car had gone round the corner, Jane turned and started walking off without a word. I stood watching her, she was moving slowly — you can catch me up if you want to — but I didn't want to, I needed to be on my own, and instead of following her, I went off left down another road, and into a pub I knew.

The landlord said, 'Well, well, long time no see.' He was a big fellow who used to be a boxer, in fact there was a picture of him hanging up behind the bar, pulling a face over his boxing gloves, and looking about five stone lighter. I said, 'Yes, it is, isn't it?' Jane didn't like pubs; she'd come, but it was under sufferance. She wanted me home, in the little nest, where I was all hers and she could keep an eye on me. The landlord asked, 'What'll it be? Pint of bitter? I shall draw it for you myself,' and he did. I took it, and went to a table in the corner; I wasn't in the mood for a patter act. He called after me, 'Cheer up! She may have got the dates wrong!'

I finished the beer, and bought a double whisky; by now the landlord had gone round to the public bar, thank God, you could hear him laughing like a drain at some feeble joke he'd made. I wanted to get drunk, I knew what was waiting for me in the flat; tears, how could you? you don't love me — and I just couldn't face it. I thought, Jesus, I can never get away from her, least of all in my own flat, the one place where I used to be able to get away from anybody. And I felt this rage with her, I wanted to ring up and shout, 'Fuck off out of my flat! If you're there when I get back, I'll kick you out!' I even went to the phone, but when the pennies had clunked into the slot, it was John I rang, not Jane.

He sounded surprised to hear me. I said, 'I'm in a pub. Come over and have a drink.' He said, 'Now?' I said, 'Yes, *now*! There's still three-quarters-of-an-hour to closing time. I'm in the Cromwell.' He'd been in here with me before. He said, 'Why don't you come here? We can drink for as long as you like.' I said, 'No: here,' and in the end he agreed.

When he arrived, he didn't see me at first. He came in in this tentative, disapproving way of his, very upright, head turning and bobbing from side to side like a supercilious ostrich, or even, it was cruel of me to think so, a pantomime dame. The landlord was back again, and he pointed me out from behind the bar, 'Come to cheer up our friend? There he is; the one by himself in the corner.'

John turned then and came over, standing above the table, looking down at me with his half-smile. I said, 'For Christ's sake get yourself a drink, and sit down.' He said, 'And you?' I said, 'You can get me another whisky.' He stood a moment, looking at me, but then he gave a double nod, still smiling, and went over to the bar. When he got back with the drinks—he'd bought himself a Pim's—I said, 'Her mother came.' He said, 'I see.' I said, 'You don't see. You've got no bloody idea.' He said, 'Very well. I don't see.' I said, 'Lady Muck. Looking round the flat like this: as though she thought there'd be coal in the bath. Jesus. Who bloody well asked her?' He said, '*Some*body must have done, presumably.' I said, '*She* did. Who do you think? Jane. A tour of bloody inspection. What would I look like in my native surroundings?'

He said, 'And I suppose you were terribly rude to her.' I said, 'Not rude. I just stopped speaking to the old cow,' and he said, 'Well ... ' raising his eyebrows. I said, 'What am I meant to do? Behave as if I think I'm going to be her son-in-law, God help me? I'm sorry you don't like the flat, Mrs Ridding, I'm sorry you don't like my accent, Mrs Ridding, but we're getting it changed, we're getting them both changed.'

He said, 'And Jane?' I said, 'Oh, fuck Jane,' then immediately felt ashamed, and angry with her for *that*. I said, 'She's at home. At least, I suppose she is. When we'd seen her bloody mother off, I let her go. I'd had enough. I couldn't face it.' He said, '*I* see.' I said, 'No, you don't. You can't possibly see. *My* flat, and I can't even go back there; without *tears*, without *silences*. She'll probably be on the phone to Mummy right this minute: Mummy, he's left me. And a good job, too, my darling, his flat was *much* too small, and his *accent*. Bloody cow.'

He asked, 'Would you like me to ring her?' I said, 'Who?' He said, 'Jane, of course. She's bound to be worried.' I said, 'She bloody well ought to be worried, she'll be lucky if I go back at all.' He shrugged and said, 'Well, if you want to sleep on my sofa ... ' I said, 'Yes, I do,' and the big clot behind the bar shouted, 'Time, gentlemen, *if* you please.'

I got up and the whisky hit me, John had to catch hold of me, but out in the air, I felt a little better. He said, 'Well, my car's round the corner, that's if you're *sure*.' I said, 'Oh, Christ, I suppose we'd better go back and tell her, first. Come with me.' He stopped and he said, 'Do you think that's a good idea?' I said, 'Why the hell not? *And* we'll have a drink, first. It's my flat, you're my bloody friend. If she wants to stay, she'll have to get used to it.' He said, 'Oh, well. I suppose you'd never get there, alone.'

He took my arm and we walked it, we got to my door and I'd forgotten the key. I went through pocket after pocket, with John fretting there beside me, till I said, 'It's no good. I'll have to ring the bell.' He said, 'Well, I think perhaps I ought to go.' I said, 'No! Stay! I'm coming back with you.' He said, 'Don't you think that now you're here ... ' I said, 'I think the same. Exactly the same. I'm inviting you. It's my flat. I put up with her mother, didn't I?' I heard him murmur, 'Did you?' then he said, in a normal voice, 'I still think you'd be better without third parties; especially me,' but I jammed my finger on the bell and kept it there. I kept on pushing, till he said, 'Geoff!' and put his hand on my arm, then I gave it another half-minute or so, and stopped.

Listening, I could hear her coming down the stairs, now, slop-slop, her slippers against the lino, and John must have heard it, too. Even though I was drunk, I could tell he was petrified; for a moment I thought he'd turn tail, and I grabbed his sleeve. Then the door opened and there she was, Lady Macbeth without the candle, in her dressing-gown, with a net round her hair. When she saw the two of us, her mouth twitched. We looked at one another, her eyes had gone quite dead, though they were red with crying, too. All she said was, 'You'd better come in.' John started, 'Now you're here ... ' but I said, 'You're coming in, too.' He said, 'It's dreadfully late,' looking at Jane, but she just said, in the same dead voice, 'If Geoff wants you to.' I said, 'I do,' and she led the way up the stairs, then John, looking round now and then, with his eyebrows raised, then me. As we got into the flat she said, 'I'm going back to bed,' and off she went, not looking at John. I said, 'Well, go, then,' and got out the whisky in the living-room. John stood there in his overcoat and said, 'I *must* go, Geoff.' I said, 'No, sit down, you're going to have a drink. People come here, and she thinks she can freeze them out; but not her bloody mother.' He said, 'I've really had enough. We've both had enough. Good luck. I'll ring you in the morning,' and he slipped out of the door.

I followed him through it, through the front door, too; I called after him down the well of the stairs, but the way I felt, I didn't fancy going down them on my own. So there was nothing to do but go back and have another whisky, then another, and I was just finishing that when in she came, Lady Macbeth again, though by now I wasn't seeing all that clearly. She said, 'Don't you think you'd better come to bed?' I said, 'Me? You mind your own bloody business.' She said, 'Come on,' and took me by the arm.

I didn't struggle, to tell the truth, I needed to lie down, the bloody room was coming and going, and in the bedroom I pitched straight across the bed while she took off my shoes, then my trousers, my socks, my shirt; then, when she'd undressed me, helped me on with my pyjamas. God, how she loved playing hospitals.

I went to sleep at once, and when I woke up, she wasn't there. I sat up with a jerk, and a pain seared through my head like the flame of a blow torch. When I looked at my watch, it said half past ten. I couldn't remember all that happened, just that there'd been this blow up, and with John in it, that she might have done something drastic. I looked round the room, but nothing seemed to have changed, her clothes were obviously still here; no note on the bedside table, none in the living-room, when I'd staggered in there. I sat down on the sofa with my head in my hands, trying to fit the pieces together, working from this memory of the row to what had actually happened, and the more I remembered, the worse it got. I remembered her mother coming, then leaving her in the street, then the pub, then John, then — Jesus! — coming back with John.

For a moment I thought of phoning her, then I thought hell, why should I? I had to make a stand sooner or later, that was what last night had been about. But although I knew this, I didn't feel it as strongly as I had last night; in fact the only thing I felt strongly was my bloody headache.

But while I was thinking should I, shouldn't I, and wondering what mood she'd be in, now, the phone went, and it was her.

She said, 'Are you all right?' quite solicitous, no different from usual, and that surprised me. In fact to tell the truth, I felt a bit relieved, as well. I said, 'Oh, pretty lousy. A hell of a bloody headache,' and she said, 'Poor thing. Take some Codeine. I thought I'd better let you sleep. Have you had any breakfast?'

So there we were, friends again, or so we seemed to be. I sat there a while trying to work it out, but then gave up. What the hell? John rang after that: was everything all right, obviously bursting to know, half hoping it wouldn't be, half hoping he wasn't in the shit. I said, 'Yes, as far as I can tell.' He said, 'I suppose she's absolutely furious with me?' I said, 'I don't think so. I don't think she's furious with anybody. God knows.' He said, 'Well, *that's* good,' but sounded rather disappointed. He said, 'Anyway, there's rather good news.' I said, 'About what?' He said, 'About the book. There's *film* interest!' I said, 'In the *camel*.' He said, 'Yes, believe it or not, in the camel; in America,' and I thought he was joking, I said, 'With Cary Grant as the back end, I suppose, and Marlon Brando in the front.' He said, 'For car*toons*. Apparently there's a man who was shown the proofs in New York; he'll be in London later this month, and he wants to see us.' I said, 'I'll believe it when I see it.' John said, 'Well, it *sounds* quite promising,' and I realised he was peeved, but I wasn't up to helping him build castles in the air, least of all with a hangover.

I spent the day recovering, I only went out for a packet of cigarettes, late in the afternoon. When Jane came back, I had my feet up on the sofa. She said, 'How *are* you?' very concerned, and I noticed she was carrying two or three parcels. She handed the smallest to me and said, 'I bought you some handkerchiefs, you need them,' and there they were, three silk handkerchiefs, all with G on them, a peace offering, but *why*? I said, 'Thank you, darling,' and gave her a kiss.' She said, 'I'm sorry about last night.' I said, '*You*? Why should you be?' She said, 'It was Mummy. I just don't seem to be able to help myself, she has this effect on me. She dominates me; while I'm with her, I seem to see everything from her point of view.' I shrugged; I'd got nothing to say. She said, 'You, darling, the flat, everything. I lay awake nearly all night, thinking about it.'

I said, 'I wasn't exactly polite to her.' She said, 'But I know exactly how you felt,' and she looked at me with her eyes wide, like two great dark pools of sincerity that you could drown in. She said, 'Mummy's so used to just riding over people that she's always amazed when they stand up to her. She can't understand why anyone should disagree with her. She phoned me at the office today, but I told her I was busy, I couldn't speak to her.' I said, 'I see,' though in fact I was baffled. I suppose she thought I must still be choked, because she sat down beside me, putting her cheek against mine, and said, 'I've been miserable all day.' I said, 'I'm sorry.' She said, 'You're quite right, I know I ought to stand up to them, but it's terribly hard.' I said, 'It must be.' She ran her fingers through my hair and said, 'I can do it, if you help me.' I said, 'Good,' and then she said, 'You *will* help me, won't you, Geoff?' I said, 'Yes, if I can.'

When we got to bed, I wanted to sleep, she wanted to make love. I'd turned my back to her, but she kept whispering, 'Geoff, Geoff, are you awake?' knowing damn well I was; so in the end I gave in and made love to her for the sake of peace and quiet. When she came, it was with a great, rushing sigh. It seemed more than just grateful; it sounded almost as if she thought she'd won a race.

CHAPTER EIGHT

One evening the phone went and an American voice said, 'Is that Geoffrey Barnes? Hi! Your camel is great!' and I thought it must be someone having me on, I said in *my* American voice, 'It's great of you to call and say so.' There was a bit of a pause, and then he said, 'No, but I really mean it. I told your friend: Disney, Schmisney, this is something absolutely new. For the first time, animals are being treated as intelligent human beings. I've worked in movies, I've worked in television, I've worked in comic books, and I know what I'm saying,' and I got a bit worried, because this sounded genuine, then I remembered John had told me some American was coming.

So I said in my normal voice, 'I don't think I quite got your name.' He said, 'Hal Kaplan. And I am a movie producer and I want the three of us to get together and work out a deal based on mutual integrity and mutual respect.' I said, 'Great … ' He said, 'You know what? This camel of yours is a very sympathetic figure. I see it in a series of ten-minute black-and-white television films. Because this is the age of the cartoon animal on television: Yogi Bear, Top Cat, Snaggle Puss; but these characters are all grotesque. Yours has dignity.'

I still couldn't quite believe it, but you didn't get time to think, the words rolled on and on and took you with them. It was only when he said, 'Okay, Geoff, take it easy, I'll be calling you again,' and rang off, that I could collect my thoughts, and wonder whether he was off his head.

I rang John, and he'd had the same treatment. He said, 'I don't believe in him either, but he's staying at the Savoy. I suppose that means something.' I said in my American voice, 'He thinks our camel has a hell of a lot of dignity,' and John said, 'Well, you never *know*.'

We met him a couple of days later, in the foyer of the Savoy. I liked being there, I always have liked the posh hotels, their sort of reverent atmosphere of money; those women in furs and smooth men smelling of toilet water and thick carpets and deferential porters. I didn't envy these people and I didn't admire them; I suppose I just liked the feeling that these places would be there for *me*, some day or other, if I ever made it, and if I couldn't afford them now, the next best thing was being invited.

But the first thing Kaplan said when he came hurrying up to us was, 'Let's go out and eat. This place is beginning to bug me.'

He didn't look at us much, when he talked. There seemed to be a great head of steam building up inside him all the time. He was always worried, always distracted; if he sat down one moment he'd be up the next, pacing around again. He had a very dark, intense face, Jewish, I suppose, with short, black hair, brooding eyes, and a long nose. When he straightened up, he had quite broad shoulders, but most of the time, he stooped; in fact his posture, when you noticed it, was a bit of a shock; it made him seem almost pathetic, till he started talking. You got the feeling he spent most of his life indoors and on the telephone.

Outside, in the Strand, he asked, 'You guys know anywhere good?' which rather shook us. Besides, how did you answer that? 'Yes: Boulestin's,' or, 'Yes, Rules,' they were both near, but now we'd left the Savoy, I'd no idea how he was thinking. He said, 'Maybe a good pub. Pubs I like,' and in the end that was what we found; a pub, in one of those streets running down to the Embankment. We had steak-and-kidney pie with boiled potatoes and the speciality of the house, soggy cabbage, and he said, 'Listen, the Savoy it isn't, but look how quick they bring it to you.' John said, 'Yes, I think they have it ready,' but he didn't react.

He said, 'So listen, let me give you my ideas. We form a company, the three of us. We call it any name you like. Maybe Camel Productions. *I* don't know. We're three equal partners, we share all profits. When we sign the contract, I make you an advance of forty thousand dollars between you. Is that fair or is it not?' John said, 'It sounds *very* fair,' which seemed to offend him. He said, '*Sounds* fair? It *is* fair. What could be fairer than equality?' and he stretched out his hand, palm upwards; yards of white cuff, thick gold cufflinks, a gold watch on a gold bracelet. I caught the Savoy smell, the toilet-water smell, yet I had a feeling he was just like me; he hadn't been born into the toilet-water world, he'd got there.

He said, 'One thing I don't like hearing: agents. You fix a good deal, everybody's happy, and the agent comes in and screws it up. He has to justify himself.' While he went on, I caught John's eye, but Hal didn't notice, there was obviously a lot he didn't notice, least of all when he was talking. Looking at him now, with his shoulders humped in his green sports coat, he reminded me of a tortoise, with his head bobbing frantically in and out of his shell; very quick, but still a tortoise. He said, 'I've already spoken to two companies out on the coast, and to their offices here in London. I've offered them a package: the book, the writer, the artist, the producer. Animation I'll take care of when we sign. And they loved it, both of them. They said they thought it sounded a great idea. And I like you. I like both of you. I think we can work together. There's only one thing.' I took the cue and asked, 'What?'

He said, 'I'm prepared to dedicate myself to this idea. To your camel. But I have to be protected. I have to know that when I come to you and say, "Hey, I've got a deal," you don't turn around and tell me, "Great, so what do we need *you* for?" '

We said no, no, we'd never dream of doing that, but it seemed to have reminded him of something, because he went straight back into his shell, all morose, and for at least a minute he said nothing at all. I looked at John again and he raised his eyebrows. The whole thing seemed so unreal. Then Hal suddenly came to life and said, 'Okay, my friends; we understand each other. Are you married? No? Neither of you? You know what? You're missing something. Here, let me show you,' and he did; photographs, his wife, back in Los Angeles, blonde and quite pretty, his two little daughters. He said, 'Kids are something everyone should have. I mean it. Do you know something? I think they're here to stay,' and he laughed like a drain and called for the bill.

Outside in the street, he took both of us by the arm, he said, 'I like London. Maybe I'll come and live here. Yeah. That may be a good idea. In Los Angeles, all you ever breathe is smog,' and we walked him back to the Savoy. At the entrance, he said, 'Okay, then, you'll be hearing from me; take it easy,' and he disappeared through all the glass and silver.

We did hear from him, too; three or four times a day, till I dreaded picking up the telephone. He might have something definite to say like, 'Geoff: hi. I have a title for us. "The Hip Camel". Is that a good title?' I'd say, 'Yes, not bad.' But mostly he just phoned. He'd say, 'Well, my friend,' in a distracted voice, almost as if I'd phoned *him*, then he'd ask, 'What have you got to tell me?' and I'd have nothing to tell him; the ball was in his court, for God's sake. John and I used to imitate him, we'd both outwardly be very sceptical, yet secretly, I think we both hoped he was going to come through with something. John had talked to our agent about him, and the agent had said, 'Be careful, he sounds like an operator. He should have made contact with me first, anyway. Don't sign anything without letting me see it.' On the other hand, as I said to John, they were all operators, it went with the territory, and you couldn't deny the energy he had, the enthusiasm, all the people he seemed to know: Disney, Houston, Presley, Brando.

One evening, he came over to us for a drink. He dug Jane, that was obvious from the moment he met her; he said, 'How do you do, and congratulations.' She smiled and asked him, 'Why?' and he said, 'Not to you, to him. For having somebody around as good-looking as you. How does he do it? What hold has he got?' She said, 'None,' and he said, 'I don't believe it. For years he's been promising to get you into pictures, and he never will. Face it. How could a pretty girl like you play a camel?'

I could see she didn't know quite how to take all this, I didn't blame her, but she laughed again—her ha-ha-ha little girl laugh—then when he was taking off his coat with his back to us she looked at me for help and I made a face: it's just the way he goes on.

Later, when she'd gone out of the room to make coffee, he asked me, 'So why don't you marry her?' I said, 'Why should I?' I was entitled to be angry, but there was something about him that always stopped me; I suppose that's how he got away with it, everywhere. He said, 'Why should you? Because she's pretty and she's nice and she loves you, that's why. Take my advice. Do it. Be decisive. Would you call yourself a decisive person?' I said, 'I don't know. I've never thought about it.' I wasn't going in for true confessions. He gave me a probing look and said, 'I'm not too sure. Sometimes, my friend, you give me the impression that you hesitate. Don't hesitate. Marry her.' I said, 'I'll have to think about it,' then, thank God, Jane came back.

He took a sip from his cup and said, 'This is great coffee,' but expressionless, as though somebody had pressed a button. He talked a bit about *The Inquisitive Camel*, he asked Jane, 'Have you read it? Don't you think it's terrific?' She said, 'I think it's very good.' He said, 'It's more than good, it's terrific,' and put his hands together, communing with himself again; or with the camel. Jane said, 'I think his play's better,' and he snapped out of his trance, he said, 'His play. You've written a play? You never told me.' I said, 'Didn't I?' I'd meant to tell Jane for Christ's sake don't bring it up. He said, 'That's right. You were an actor, weren't you? What could be more natural? Every actor thinks he can write a play. What have you done with it?' I said, 'Nothing.' He said, 'Show it to me. Maybe I can do something with it. What's it about?' I said, 'Oh, nothing much; just a send-up of modern art,' then Jane came charging in, explaining, getting most of it wrong, but he hardly seemed to listen, he said, 'Yeah, that's funny ... I like that ... that's very funny,' in his press-button style, and after she'd been going a couple of minutes, he got up and started wandering round the room, pulling books halfway out of the shelves, then letting them fall back again, lifting up china ornaments Jane had brought with her, still saying, 'That's good ... that's really funny ... that's good,' until I couldn't decide which of the two of them was irritating me most.

He suddenly cut in and said, 'I called my wife today, in California. You know what? My younger kid said, "Daddy, I miss you." At two years old. Is that remarkable? "Daddy, I miss you." ' Jane said, 'Sweet,' and I took the chance to leap in and say, 'Anyway, the play isn't finished, yet; I'll show it to you when it is,' and he said, 'Fine,' obviously as glad to let it drop as I was.

When he'd gone at last, Jane said, 'Be careful, Geoff,' very earnest; the gypsy's warning. I asked, 'Why, didn't you like him?' and she said, 'He worried me, he's so restless. I didn't believe half he said.' I said, 'Nor does he, probably; it's part of the act. I met one or two like him when I was in the theatre.' She said, 'I just don't want him to build up all your hopes.' I said, 'Don't worry, he won't. John and I just look on it as a bit of a joke.' She said, 'As long as you're sure.' I said, 'Of course I'm sure. If it came off, it would be a miracle.'

Our agent did some checking and found out Hal *had* worked on at least a couple of television series; as assistant producer, things like that. He said, 'He's wheeling and dealing,' and when I went to Hal's room at the Savoy, I saw what he meant. I never talked to him for more than a minute at a time; either the phone rang, or else he picked it up, himself: 'How's my Paris number? ... I want you to get me Los Angeles ... Call me the Paramount office ... get me Twentieth Century-Fox.'

Once he looked up from the phone and said, 'Did you bring that play of yours along?' I said, 'No.' He said, 'Bring it. Never mind finishing it. You can't tell. Maybe you should be writing it as a picture.' All over the room, there were screenplays in those blue-and-green cardboard covers, with a cellophane panel for the title, kid's comics, children's books, like ours was going to be. He said, 'Forget the stage, my friend, you're going to write for the movies. You have a fine sense of a story. I'm not kidding. In those cartoon films, the story line is what makes it, and *you* found the story line, your friend just drew the pictures. Am I right?' I said, 'More or less.' He said, 'Don't be so loyal; you know I'm a hundred per cent right. Anyway, he draws well, we can use him.' Then the phone rang again.

This time, his tone changed, even his expression changed. He was dead serious now, off on a completely different pitch, he said, 'Listen, I assure you the film I intend to make from *The Wind in the Willows* will be a dignified, important film. It will be made with integrity. It will be absolutely faithful to the story.' Afterwards he said, 'Those schnooks, they guard these fucking books like it was their daughter's virginity. Do you know *The Wind in the Willows*? Do you think you could adapt it? I *know* you could adapt it. Okay, so don't waste time. There's a copy there on that table. Take it home with you, work me out a story line,' then before I could say yes or no, he was on the line to New York.

After that, he tried to get Sir Laurence Olivier. He said to me, 'I want him to be Toad. Is that a great idea?' and when he was obviously told to hang on, he turned to me again and said, 'Listen, don't get offended. Your friend John; is he a fag?' I said, 'Perhaps. I've never asked him.' He said, 'You British amuse me, you're so goddam reticent. You never asked him! That's good! Who needs to ask him? It stands out a mile, but what the hell does it matter? He's a very sweet guy. I just wanted to be sure.'

I was irritated but I didn't want him to see it, because I knew that would mean more probing, so I waited till he'd been told Olivier couldn't speak to him, then said that I had to rush off to a lunch appointment. He said, 'You have too many lunch appointments. Do you want to know something? You're carrying too much weight. I mean it. It isn't good. More exercise, less lunch appointments. Be decisive. Okay, then. Tomorrow I go to Rome. Maybe when I get back there'll be news for us. And read *The Wind in the Willows*; I'm serious, we could both be rich.'

CHAPTER NINE

———◆◆◆———

I'd expected ructions after Jane's mother came, and of course we had them; marathon phone calls to Jane that left her wrung out and weepy — I said, 'Why can't you hang up on her, for God's sake?' — then, one day, a phone call from her old man to me. He said, 'Look, I wonder if you'd come to my club and have lunch with me?' For a moment I felt like saying, 'No, I wouldn't,' and putting down the phone, I resented the way they'd all put me on the spot, but then I agreed; in a strange way, I felt sorry for him. He was obviously just firing more bullets that she'd made for him. So I said, 'All right,' and we fixed it.

I hate clubs, the few I've ever been to. I don't mind being what I am, but I dislike the way they drive it home to me; I'd think of the Groucho Marx line, 'I wouldn't join a club that would have me for a member,' but none of these clubs would ever have me for a member; that was one of the things they were there for. You'd think while you were inside them that nothing had changed since 1900; that we still had India, Queen Victoria was on the throne, and the lower classes knew their places.

He fitted it perfectly, he really belonged there; far more than he did at home. The club was off Piccadilly, a big, white stucco building with a portico; he was waiting in the lobby and he asked me, 'Ever been here before?' I said, 'No,' which was a mistake, because he led me off on a conducted tour, room after room where nothing was happening; billiard tables that weren't being used, a gloomy library full of books that never got read, a smoking-room with one thin old man asleep in a leather chair, a reading-room where more old men were dozing over newspapers or strutting across the carpet like storks, to change one paper for another.

He introduced me to one of them, a dark man in spectacles with a stoop and a rather surprising expression; not the usual blue glaze, more like a kind old woman in spectacles. Ridding said, 'George, I want you to meet Mr Geoffrey ... ' then forgot my name. For a moment I let him stand there gulping like a fish, then I told him, 'Barnes,' and he said, 'That's right, Barnes!' as if it was I, not him, who'd forgotten. The brown old man asked, 'Any relation of Mr Justice Barnes?' and I almost said yes, just to see the effect on Ridding, but I said, 'No.' He said, 'Aren't you? Brilliant mind. Better known for his *obiter dicta* than his judgments,' and of course the corridors were full of all the usual Spy cartoons of judges, lawyers, Empire Builders.

Ridding took me through them to the dining-room, light at last, like coming out of one of those tiny medieval Italian alleys, into a blazing square. There were tall windows overlooking the street, and a long, polished table down the middle of the room which seemed to be the convivial table, where people could pretend they were back in the mess again or even at public school; there was a lot of heavy laughing going on. We sat at a table by the window, and a waiter in a red linen jacket came up doing the faithful old retainer bit, 'Not the beef today I wouldn't, sir.' 'No? No? What's the matter with it, Parkin?' '*Well*, sir, in my opinion, it's seen slightly better days.'

So we ordered tomato soup, then lamb, neither of which was any good; the lamb was stringy and the soup could have come out of a tin, and Mr Ridding threshed around trying to find things to talk about before he had to come

125

to the point. Mostly he talked about stocks and shares, saying every now and then, 'Don't know if this sort of thing interests you at all?' but it did, I'd never had a stock or a share in my life, but I liked to hear about it; it was like being in a foreign country, where you knew just enough of the language to get by. 'Jumped five shillings overnight when word got round of Clore's takeover bid ... in the end, though, the bears had the last word ... I said at the time the fellow was running a glorified bucket shop, you simply can't *do* that sort of thing without adequate capital.'

I thought, adequate capital; what would he say if he knew Jane had been paying my rent?

At last he looked into his coffee cup and said in an almost apologetic voice, 'Look here, I thought I ought to have a word with you about Jane.' I felt very weary when I heard that, I said, 'Yes, I see.' He said, 'Her mother's a bit worried. I mean to say, if the two of you want to live together before you get married, I suppose that's *your* affair, but we'd feel much happier if we could set a date.' And something blew, like a fuse; suddenly I felt hemmed in by them, they were cutting me off, suffocating me, moving in closer and closer. I said, 'There *isn't* a date.'

He said, 'What?' It had obviously rocked him on his heels. I said, 'There isn't any date.' He said, 'But Jane told my wife ... I understood the autumn.' I said, 'It's news to me.' That shut him up completely, but I didn't help him out. *I'd* never told them any date, *I'd* never made them any promises, it wasn't for me to start explaining. At last he said, 'You are *getting* married?' and I told him, 'I don't know,' which stopped him dead again. When he did speak, he was almost spluttering, he could hardly get the words out; he said, 'You don't ... you're not ... ' and then, 'I don't understand.'

I couldn't look at him, I said, 'It's simple enough. We

may get married, we may not, that's all.' At least I could give him that much. He gulped like a fish again, and said, 'This will come as a terrible shock to her mother.' I said, 'I'm sorry.' He said, 'You mean to tell me Jane's been lying to us all this time, telling us the wedding was as good as fixed?' I said, 'Maybe she misunderstood.' He said, 'How *could* she misunderstand? Either she hasn't been telling us the truth, or you've led her to believe you'd marry her.' I said, 'I don't know what she's told you. I've never led her to believe anything.'

He said, 'I'm afraid I must insist that she leave your flat at once,' and I saw red again, I asked him, 'What do you mean, insist?' He said, 'I'm her father.' I said, 'What if you are? You can't compel her; she's got a right to make her own decisions.' He said, 'I realise the present position must suit you extremely well,' which made me angrier still; I said, 'What do *you* know about it?' and he gave a nervous glance at the middle table where the booming and haw-hawing had stopped, and they were obviously listening, but I didn't lower my voice, it was his own damn fault. I said, 'You haven't got the first idea what goes on between Jane and myself. *I'm* not trying to hang on to her. If she told me she wanted to leave, I'd let her go tomorrow; but she doesn't.' He said, 'No, precisely, that's why somebody has to see to it that she does, before there's serious damage done.'

I felt like saying, oh, take her away if you want to, see if it worries *me*, but it wouldn't have been fair to Jane; after all, I did owe her something, and besides, he'd really annoyed me; so I said, 'I suppose you'll make life hell for her, till she does what you want.' He said, 'What the devil do you mean?' so loud that it scared him and he dropped his voice almost to a whisper, making me want to laugh; 'what do you mean?' The old boys at the long table were practically falling off their chairs by now; they couldn't have had a sideshow like this since Mafeking Night. I said, '*You* know what I mean. You'll pester her and bully her until she gives in; that's been the trouble all along.' The blood came into his face; he said in a low, shaking voice, 'I have *never* been spoken to like this.' I shrugged, I said, 'Look, Mr Ridding, I know I'm not the son-in-law you want. I don't look right, I don't sound right, I haven't been to the right school and I don't do the right job. I'd have thought you'd be glad to know I shan't be marrying Jane. But if I were in *your* shoes, I'd keep clear of it and let things work themselves out. People *have* affairs; we're living in the nineteen-sixties. People *do* live together. Then they stop living together. Jane isn't old. She won't go on the shelf when she leaves me.' (I thought, or when I leave *her*.) He was still glaring at me apoplectically, but at last all he said was, 'We'd better have our coffee next door.'

Next door was the reading-room; you filed past a trolley and poured your own coffee, very democratic—which was about as good as the meal had been. When we sat down, another of his friends came up and he had to introduce me again, he did it almost without looking at me, then, thank God, the friend sat down with us and I was able to leave them to it, saying that I'd got an appointment. He said, 'I see, very well, then, goodbye,' then the old conditioning took over and he stood up and shook hands with me. Dismissed.

Out in the street, it felt as if I'd escaped from a tomb. As soon as I passed a phone box, I went into it and rang Jane. I said, 'Prepare yourself for the Blitzkrieg.' She said, 'Oh, darling, didn't it go well?' and I said, 'What did you expect?' She said, 'You weren't rude to him?' I said, 'I told him the truth, that's all,' and she said, 'But what did he *say*? What did he want us to do?' I said, 'Get married. I told him we hadn't any plans, and they ought to let you make your own decisions.' There was a silence, then she said, in a dull, flat voice, 'I see. And what did he say to that?' I said, 'What you'd expect. He went up in flames.' Another pause. She said, 'I suppose it's *my* fault.' I said, 'It's *not* your fault! When are you going to get that out of your head? If you want to live with me, you live with me. You don't have to explain it to them.' She said, 'Yes, I know,' in the same pale voice, and I said, 'Cheer up, I'll see you tonight,' then put the phone down. It *was* her fault, but why tell her so?

That evening she came back in tears, her mother had been on to her already; why hadn't she told them the truth, how could she do such a thing, couldn't she see I was taking advantage of her? Then, round about ten, it was her father, I sat by her and listened to the whole thing; she was disgracing them, it wasn't even as if I were able to support her, didn't she realise she was simply making a fool of herself?

Every now and then she looked at me with a sort of despair, then she'd say, 'Yes, Daddy, no, Daddy.' When she'd rung off I said, 'Why don't you stand up to him?' She said, 'It's so difficult.' I said, 'It's easy. All you've got to say is, it's my life, I'll do what I want with it,' and she said, 'Yes, it's easy for *you*,' and she cried, she came into my arms. I patted her head, I stroked her, I said, 'For God's sake, you're grown up; why should *they* run your life?' feeling guilty all the time because I still couldn't offer her what I knew she wanted. She said, 'Oh, you're right, you're right, I know you're right,' and went on crying. So there I was, enlisted on her side against *them*. If I took a step back, it looked ridiculous, but what could I do? She was right, they were wrong, and some day she had to break away from them.

CHAPTER TEN

Then there was Rosemary. She'd been strange for weeks, the way women get when they're cooling off, so that there's always a reasonable explanation for everything, yet you know deep down that none of them holds water. She'd say, 'Can't talk to you now, darling,' in a stage whisper, when I phoned, or she'd arrange to come round and not turn up —there was always a good excuse. Once she asked me to her place, and when I arrived, there was nobody in. *I* knew. She was telling me, get rid of Jane, and how could I get rid of Jane, at this stage? Besides, in an odd sort of way I wanted both of them, Rosemary for mistress, Jane as a sort of wife; even if I wasn't married to her, I somehow couldn't think of her as a mistress; and nor did she.

And all this time there was Hal, running through everything like a crazy theme, phoning me three or four times a day, driving me up the wall and round the bend. 'Listen, if there's someone I'm working with and I don't call him a couple of times a day, there's something wrong.' It was a strange time, a sort of phoney war; on the one hand Jane, who I didn't want to marry but was backing up as if I did; in the middle, Hal, who I was sure would never get us anywhere, but couldn't bring myself to ditch: and Rosemary.

One day at last she *did* come round, and it was great; so good that nothing might ever have gone wrong. She said, 'Oh, it's *nice* to see you again,' I put my hands on her breasts, and we were away. The phone went a couple of times while we were making love, but I was damned if I'd answer it, I knew it would be Hal Kaplan.

We made love three or four times, I was carried away, I never noticed the time, and when I did, it was twenty to six. I flew into a panic, but I didn't dare let her see. At the same time, I was sure that she guessed from the expression on her face, the way she smiled at me, and she seemed to take a delight in being slow, so that I was sitting dressed in the living-room while she was still messing around in the bathroom, wanting to run and knock on the door, telling her, 'Come on, for Christ's sake, come *on*!'

It was five to six by the time she came out. I said, 'Okay, love, I'll see you,' holding her coat all ready for her, and she turned, smiling at me, as she put her arm in the sleeve and said, 'I'm going, don't worry!' I said, 'It isn't that, you know what things are like,' and she laughed at me and said, 'I wish you could see yourself, you look just like a spaniel!' For a moment I hated her, I wanted to say fuck off, for God's sake fuck off, but I knew I still needed her, I knew she knew it too, the bitch. When I got her to the door I kissed her, saying, 'Sorry for rushing you; I'll phone you tomorrow.' She said, 'All right: if I'm in.'

When I opened the door, I heard Jane's footsteps coming up the stairs. She was still a couple of floors down, but there was no mistaking them, brisk, light, not quite running; and my stomach dissolved, my heart began thumping like a piston. Rosemary asked, 'What's the matter?' I said, 'It's her, for Christ's sake hurry, go past her without looking at her,' and she whispered back, 'All right,' not smiling, now, and went off down the stairs, while I dived back into the flat, into the living-room.

I pulled out a book and pretended to be reading it, God knows what it was, then remembered: the bathroom, and raced in there to see if she'd left anything around. I was still there when I heard Jane unlock the door, and I couldn't face her, I went over to the lavatory and had a pee, trying to work out what I'd say, waiting for her to call to me. But she didn't call, which was worse, so in the end I had to go out and face her.

She was sitting in a chair in the living-room, dead white; she scarcely looked at me, as I came in. She said in a sort of sleep-walking voice, 'Who *was* that?' I said, 'Who?' She said, 'That woman.' I was going to say, 'What woman?' but I realised it was useless; they'd obviously passed on the landing below, and there was only one flat on our floor. So I said, 'She was here for tea, that's all.' She asked in the same, flat voice, 'What's her name?' I said, 'Rosemary. I bumped into her the other day. I knew her in rep.' She said, 'You were making love to her, weren't you?' I said, 'Rubbish.' She said, 'Yes, you were, I know you were,' and the tears slid out of her eyes and down her cheeks. I knelt on the floor beside her and put my arm round her shoulders, but she stood up and shook it off, she said, 'It's no use lying.' I said, 'For Christ's bloody *sake*, I tell you I'm *not* lying,' and she said, 'The look she gave me; that was enough.' I thought the cow, the fucking cow. I said, 'Jesus, you're im*a*gining things.' She said, 'No, I'm not,' and suddenly went out of the room; before I could catch up with her she was in the bedroom and she'd locked the door.

I banged on it, I shouted, 'Jane!' but she didn't answer. I knocked again, fairly thumping on it, still no use, and when I stopped I could hear her moving about inside, shifting things, and I knew what she was doing; she was packing. I went back to the living-room and sat down, I was just paralysed, for the moment I couldn't think of a single way round it; I could only sit there till I watched her go, and I knew I didn't want her to go, I was frightened of her going. God knows how long I sat there, still frozen. At last the key turned in the bedroom lock and she came

132

to the doorway carrying one of her suitcases, her face still set in the same, blank mask. She put the case down, went straight across the room to the telephone, and ordered a radio cab. I said, 'Jane!' but she took no notice of me, just turned, went back to the door, and picked up the case again.

I got up then and went to her, pulling the case away from her, I said, 'Don't be so bloody silly, there was *nothing*,' but she said, 'Will you let me have my case?' I said, 'Jane,' but she stood there waiting, not looking at me, till I put the case down beside her and she took it up again, putting it down by the front door, opening that, picking it up, going out, closing the door behind her. No goodbye.

I didn't attempt to follow her, I felt wrung out. I walked back into the living-room for a moment, then out of there into the bedroom. Her other suitcase was still there, on top of the wardrobe, and seeing that gave me a little hope. Sooner or later she'd have to be back for it, and whatever she'd left in the cupboards and drawers. I looked, and there was quite a lot: two suits, several dresses and sweaters, three pairs of shoes, some underwear, a couple of pairs of stockings. Then, after feeling hopeful, I began to get angry; I thought fuck them, fuck both of them; Jane for walking out on me, Rosemary for deliberately provoking it. I'd like to have got hold of her and belted her, I'd never hit a woman in my life, but *she* deserved it, the bitch. At the same time there was this knowing that I'd lost her, I'd lost both of them, and I was still scared; it had come so suddenly, one-two, like that; no warning. One moment you had two girl-friends, the next you were alone. And I was afraid to be alone, of this great, black wave that one of these days would sweep over me and choke me, drown me.

I picked the phone up and rang John, I said, 'I'm coming round, okay?' He said, 'As a matter of fact, I was just going out to see a film.' I said, 'I'll pick you up, we'll go together, I'm coming now.'

In the end we didn't go, we stayed in his flat and talked; or rather, I did, I talked for hours, while he sat and listened with his usual smile, till I said to him, 'For Christ's sake, what's amusing?' and he said, 'Nothing.' I got up and started walking around, I said, 'I'm at the end of the road, I don't know what I'll do, and you just sit there, smiling. How the hell would you like it if ... ' He said, 'If what?' and I said, 'I don't know.' For a second I'd felt like saying, 'If *I* laughed when your boy-friends rang you up and upset you,' but it wouldn't be fair, and I knew he'd never forgive me. That side of his life was something you must never mention, never even seem to notice, but I think he guessed what I meant, because his smile disappeared and he said in an offended voice, 'I'm sorry if I seem unsympathetic.' I said, 'Take no notice of me, I'm upset, that's all. One-two, just like that.'

He said, 'You're sure Rosemary did it on purpose?' I said, 'Positive. The way she'd been behaving, like women do, when an affair's gone sour. They pretend to be broad-minded, but they never are. They want you exclusively. What she'd probably expected me to say was I'll give Jane up, I'll kick her out, it's only you I want.' He said, 'It's not very fair, is it?' and seemed surprised by it, as if he was discovering a strange new world, as foreign to him as his phone calls were to me. He said, 'Jane might come back,' as though he wanted to be contradicted. I said, 'Oh, she'll come back for the case; that's probably why she left it there. She wants a great forgiveness scene, me down on my knees begging her pardon, promising not to screw anyone but her again for the rest of my life. I told you, they're all the bloody same, they blackmail you, they chip away at you. What the hell do I owe her? What the hell did I ever promise her! *I* never wanted her to move in.'

He said, 'Then perhaps it's just as well she moved out.'
I said, 'Yes, but both of them together, just like that.' And
I wondered where Jane had gone, back to her parents, I
supposed, where they'd probably got the champagne out
by now. 'Damn glad to hear it. Behaved like a perfect
bounder at my club.' Fuck the lot of them. Or maybe to
Marion, just for the night: 'At last you've done the only
sensible thing.' *She'd* be delighted. I had a sudden,
ridiculous impulse to speak to Jane, at least to find out
where she was, but I killed it at once; what was the
object, even if I did? Sod her.

I said, 'You couldn't put me up on the sofa tonight?' He
said, 'Yes, of course,' and I said, 'If I go back to my place,
I'll only drink myself silly.' I was drinking now, John's
brandy—he hadn't any whisky. I said, 'I'll bring you
another bottle of this,' but he said, 'It doesn't matter.'

I had another impulse, this time to say to John, 'Why
don't we two share a flat?' but killed that, too. It might be
a sort of guarantee, against depression, against this terrible
black loneliness, against the boozing and the misery when
things went wrong like now. But I knew it wouldn't work;
John with his boy-friends, me with my birds, our two
different planets. So I had another drink and slept on his
sofa, which was bloody uncomfortable. Some time in the
night I got the feeling he was standing there in the middle
of the room, watching me, but it may have been only a
dream.

CHAPTER ELEVEN

Next morning, I went home. John said, 'Stay if you like,' but I said, 'No, I'd better go, I'll have to go back sooner or later.' At the front door he said, in an uncertain way, 'If there's anything I can do ... ' but I said, 'Nothing, thanks. There isn't much anyone can do.'

Back in the flat, I picked up her china ornaments in the living-room and threw them one by one against the wall; snap, crash; I felt better while I was doing it, but afterwards when they were lying there in pieces, the china ballerina, the china cat, the china dogs and all the members of the bloody china orchestra, I felt ashamed, I could have cried. I didn't pick them up, I felt too depressed even for that; I just turned the radio up to 'Music While You Work', or some such rubbish, and sat there with no will to do anything. When the front door bell went I thought oh, shit, let it ring, but a few seconds after it had stopped it began again, on and on and on, boring through my head, then stopped, then began *again*, so that I swore and went thundering down the stairs.

It was Marion. I asked, 'What are you trying to do, wear the bell out?' She said, 'I thought there must be no one in.' I said, 'If you thought that, why didn't you go away?' Her face was one great chunk of disapproval, like an old spinster walking through the courting couples in Hyde Park. She said, 'I've come for the rest of Jane's clothes.' I said, 'Have you? Why couldn't she come, herself?' She said, 'I should have thought that was fairly obvious.' I said, 'My God you're enjoying this, aren't you?' but she ignored me again and said, 'Are you going to let me in or not?' I let out a sigh and I said, 'Yes, I suppose so.'

I stood aside to let her pass, then followed her up the stairs. She had big, plump, solid legs: I started wondering what she'd do if I suddenly reached out and pinched one of them; or even ran my hand up her thigh. I could imagine what it would be like: huge and white, rubbery. Jane still kept saying she had lovely eyes. I thought, she needs them.

Up in the flat, I steered her away from the living-room, into the bedroom. I said, 'There's the case, up there on top of the wardrobe,' and she said, '*Thank* you,' so I shrugged and got it down. I said, 'You wouldn't like me to pack it for you, would you?' and she said, 'That won't be necessary, thank you.' What a lovely sense of humour.

I left her to it and went out, into the living-room, picking up all the bits of china, burrowing under chairs and tables and the sofa for them, dropping them into the wastepaper basket. I was picking up one of the last pieces when she came in behind me and asked, 'Could you tell me where her umbrella is?' I said, 'In the cupboard in the hall,' not turning round, but she didn't go, she said, 'How did this get broken?' and my stomach flipped, I said, 'What?' She said, 'Look. This china cat. I gave it her myself, last Christmas,' and looking round, I saw it lying by her foot, a tiny piece of blue-and-white spotted china, which the pattern of the carpet must have camouflaged.

I said, 'I've no idea, it's probably been there for days,' and I got up, with the other bit of china in my hand, standing between her and the wastepaper basket. She gave me a suspicious look, obviously wanting to ask me, was it you? then she said, 'She particularly wanted all her china ornaments; do you know where I can find them?' I said,

'As a matter of fact I haven't seen them, I had an idea she'd taken them away with her.' She said, 'Well, she didn't,' and for a moment we looked at one another, me deadpan, her with this accusing expression, then, without speaking, she came farther into the room and started looking round. I said, 'I told you, they're not *in* here,' but she took no notice, I'd like to have thumped her, so I waited till she was facing the bookshelves, with her back to me, picked up the wastepaper basket, and walked out of the room.

She fairly whirled round as I came past her, but I got out of the door and into the kitchen. There I wrapped the pieces of china up in newspaper and stuffed them all into the trash pail; it was almost like burying a corpse. She followed me again and said, 'I still can't find them,' in a you-know-why-too voice. I said, 'Well, what do you want *me* to do? Conjure them up, out of thin air?' She gave me a look and said, 'Charming,' then went back to the living-room. I stood there in the kitchen seething, loathing both of them, knowing what a kick she must be getting out of this. I felt like going after her and grabbing her, shoving her through the front door, pitching the bloody case out after her. At the same time I wanted to find things out from her: what Jane had said to her, whether it was really final, so when I did go into the living-room I just stood in the doorway watching her, like she'd watched me—she ignored me, too—until I said, 'She's with you, then.' She said, without looking at me, 'For the moment.' I said, 'Not back to Mummy.' She said, 'No,' and I said, 'Wonderful; that's something, anyway,' then I asked, 'Has she told them, yet?' She said, 'I've no idea,' which to me meant, no. I said, 'All this must make you very happy.' She said, 'I'm happy for Jane, yes,' and I saw red, I said, 'You bloody hypocrite.'

She turned on me then, saying, '*What* do you mean?' I

138

said, 'I mean you're happy for yourself, not for her.' She said, 'I'm happy she's got away from *you*, at last!' I said, 'It's got nothing to do with me. It could be me or anybody else; you just want her back again on your level.' Her face was the colour of chalk, she glared at me a moment as if she'd like to kill me, then suddenly she crumpled, very ugly, and she burst into tears. She said, 'Why are you so cruel? Why do you say these things?' and then I felt sorry. I said, 'I'll get you a drink,' it was all I could think of. I didn't want to put my arms round her, to find myself comforting another bloody woman; in any case I didn't fancy her; I was sure her shoulders would be thick, and that she'd have a broad, fat arm. She said, 'I don't want a drink.' I said, 'Okay, then, a cup of tea,' and went out to the kitchen to make it; escaping, too, I suppose.

When I got back with two cups of tea, she was sitting in a chair. She'd stopped crying, but now her face was red, she was dabbing at her nose with a tiny lace handkerchief and the nose was too big, the handkerchief was too small, it looked ridiculous. I said, 'I admit I'm a swine, if that's any consolation to you.' She said, 'You've behaved disgracefully.' I said, 'What's the point of talking? We look at things from two completely different points of view.' She said, 'Yes: you're completely selfish.'

I shrugged, I said, 'What does selfish mean? We're all selfish. Jane's selfish. You're selfish.' She said, in an upstage voice, 'There are limits.' I said, 'No, there aren't; there are just different kinds of selfishness, men's and women's. My kind is that I need more than one woman. Jane's kind is she wants me all to herself.' She said, 'You've no sense of responsibility,' and I told her, 'There you go again. "You men are all the same." Well, if you ask me, you women are all the same. If we don't do what you want us to do, that means we're selfish and irresponsible.' And suddenly, with a little twinge, I thought, but not Audrey.

Out of the blue she said, 'What did you do with those china animals?' I said, 'I smashed them.' She gave me a sort of nanny look and said, 'You're just a child, aren't you?' I said, 'The party line, again. All men are children. Jesus.' She said in a crisp voice, 'Sometimes I think they are,' she seemed to be recovering. I asked her, 'Has she been crying much?' and she said, 'Quite a bit. Does that please you?' Revenge. I said, 'No, I've never wanted to make her unhappy.' She said, 'Well, you've made a pretty good job of it.' I said, 'Does your boy-friend always make *you* happy?' and her face began to break up again, then she got hold of herself and snapped, '*Very* happy!' I said, 'Okay, I'll help you down with the case, if you like,' and she gave me a suspicious look, what was I after?

Outside the house, I asked her, 'How did you get here?' She said, 'Tube; I'm going back by taxi.' I said, 'You needn't, I can drive you.' She said, 'I don't think that's necessary, thank you.' I said, 'Don't be silly. Look, there's my car. I promise I won't come up, if that's what you're worried about.' She looked at me again for a moment, then she said, 'All right. Thank you. If you're sure.' I said, 'I've got nothing much to do.'

I still wasn't certain why I'd offered to do it; guilt, perhaps, for making her cry, some vague idea of running into Jane, or possibly just hoping Marion would tell her, and it might help to bring her round. God knows.

We didn't talk much on the drive over to Canonbury, but when we did we were very polite, a sort of armed neutrality; there'd been too much said already and we both felt it. I asked her was the district still changing, and she said yes, there were more and more nice families moving in, and that sickened me, but I didn't take her up on it.

Her square was looking great, the leaves were out on the trees, now, and you could see the nice people were moving

140

in, from the Jags and the Zodiacs, the coloured front doors, the way the lace curtains were going from the windows. I said, 'Want me to help you up with the case?' She said, 'I'll manage myself, thank you.' I said, 'Come on. I'll leave it outside the door and disappear. You can tip me, if you like.'

I got out of the car and went to the boot; just as I was unlocking it, I suddenly glanced up and there she was at the window, just a glimpse of her, but definitely looking at me; and it stabbed me, like a sudden pang of hope. When I got up there, she'd open the door, maybe *be* at the door: but she wasn't; when I did get there, the door was shut. I put the case down and said, 'Well, goodbye,' and Marion said, 'Thank you,' closed and guarded, what would I do next?

All I did was go off down the stairs. Outside in the square, I looked up again, but there was no one at the window.

The phone was ringing when I got back to my flat; Hal Kaplan, all I was short of. He said, 'Geoff? Hi! I was awake at four o'clock in the morning.' I said, 'Were you?' I wasn't in the mood for playing straight man. He said, 'Four o'clock. And you know why? I was thinking. I had a great idea for us; for you and me and John. That alligator of yours; it's even more commercial than the camel. I think maybe that's what we should be working on; not the camel, the alligator. Only instead of having it in the South American jungle, we have it in the swamps of Louisiana. Like Pogo the possum. You know Pogo? He's in a strip cartoon, it's syndicated all over the United States. But listen. Hear me out. I haven't finished. This alligator is an English alligator. Is that a great idea? Then you could really handle it, you and John. An English alligator in an American swamp. I don't know. Maybe it was born at the London Zoo.'

I said, 'Terrific.' I'd had enough of his ideas. He said, 'I knew you'd have to like it. Because the camel is wonderful too, but it's got no specific American interest; your alligator is more cinematic.' I'd half switched off by now, his voice was running, running in my ear like a motor. When I switched on again, he was saying, 'So we make a company for the alligator *and* the camel; all reproduction rights. If you two are hired for the project, we split three ways, like before, with the same advance. If you don't get hired, you still get two-thirds, plus twenty thousand dollars for movie or television rights, five thousand for any others.'

I said, 'What's "any others"?' and he said, '*Any*thing else. These days, you never know. It could be comic book rights, it could be for making rubber camels. I'm being very fair to you, my friend.' I said, 'I'm sure you are.' He said, 'Okay, I'll have those contracts drawn. Shall I tell you something? You sound depressed. Why should you be depressed? You're a good-looking guy, you've got a beautiful girl-friend, you may be going to make a lot of money.' I said, 'I didn't say I was depressed.' He said, 'Talk to John about it. Tell him. I'll have my lawyers call you; we'll sign the contract. How's Jane?' I said, 'Okay.' He said, 'Don't forget what I told you: marry her.'

Putting the phone down, I had this instinct there was something wrong, but I didn't know what; at the same time I was even more depressed. The camel thing had just been a mirage, I thought, the mirage in the desert (Listen: is that a good title?) but it was something I could live with, and now there wasn't even the mirage. And I wondered, how do I pay the rent? and felt humiliated; no Jane, no camel film. When *she* was there and the mirage was there, I could tell myself, I'll pay her back, and her mirage was the play: but *now* what?

I realised again what a phoney I was, what a failure,

and what Dave said came back to me; the artist type. Jesus, how right he was. I suddenly thought I'd like to talk to him. Of all the people I knew, he seemed to see the clearest, no illusions; and I thought he might give me a line on what Hal was playing at; I was sure he was playing at something, but the figures went round in my head and didn't mean a thing.

So I phoned Dave at home, no reply, then at his television studios; he was out filming, *doing* something. Christ, I needed a girl, but these were the times you could never get one. It was all right in the old Chelsea days, a party practically every night, and nearly always some bird you could make out with. But now I was cut off, Jane had seen to that; you go domestic, and you're at their mercy.

I rang John, to talk about Hal Kaplan, and *he* couldn't make sense of it, either. He said, 'It sounds as if he wants to make the films without *us*.' I said, 'He'd still be paying us a lot of money.' John said, 'I suppose I'd better ask Mike Anstruther,' which was our agent. Later on he rang back and said, 'Mike can't understand it, either, but he says don't sign anything,' which was just as well, because ten minutes after that, some solicitor rang through and asked to what address should he send these contracts? The way I was feeling, I'd probably have signed just so as not to have Hal on the telephone.

Sitting there, I had an impulse to ring up Rosemary, I even picked up the receiver, then I thought no, to hell with her, and put it down again. In fact, three days later, it was she that called me, she said, in a cautious voice, 'Hallo. Me. Was everything all right?' I said, 'What do *you* think?' She said, 'Well, darling, don't blame *me*, I didn't plan it.' I said, 'Didn't you?' and was caught in this tug-of-war between the need to let fly at her and the need to keep her. What I said was, 'She walked out, if you really want to know.' She said, 'Oh, Geoff,' and then, 'You're not *blaming* me?' which I suppose was what she'd rung to find out. That, and to see what had happened, to know how far she'd brought it off. Well, now she knew, and I could tell it worried her.

So there I was, wanting to say fuck off, not daring to, yet still not able to tell her what she wanted: there, there, there, it wasn't your fault. The strain was too much. I plunged in, I asked her, 'When can we meet?' She said, 'Not *this* week,' in a doubtful voice. I said, 'Monday, then? Monday here?' She said, 'All right,' but I knew I hadn't handled it properly.

That Sunday, I went over to my parents. I nearly cried off, what with the questions that I knew there'd be, the explanations. In the end what made me go was just this being alone, the need to escape from it.

I just turned up, I hadn't said Jane wasn't coming, and of course right away it was, 'Where's Jane? Why haven't you brought Jane?' I said, 'Her mother's ill,' and mine said, '*Oh*, I'm sorry to hear that,' then it was Jane, Jane, Jane, right through until the end of lunch, till I thought it would drive me mad. Then, after that, the hints, the guessing, the glances; my mother getting it first, of course, as usual. And it couldn't have been too difficult, the way I felt; really down, too far down to come up, except for moments.

I was afraid Mother would get me alone and start pumping me, so I took refuge with the old man in front of the television set, pretending to watch some dreary football game. But she got me in the end, out in the garden, where I'd wandered for some air. She came after me and said, 'Geoff; you haven't quarrelled with Jane?' I said, 'Me? What makes you think that?' She said, 'Just that you seem so quiet, as if something had gone wrong.' I said, 'No, nothing has.' She said, 'That's good,' as if she didn't believe me, then, 'You're not cross with me for asking?

144

It's just that when a young girl wants to get married ... '
and I saw what she was at. I said, 'Nothing like that, at all.'

She put her arm in mine and said, 'Oh, I'm so glad,
because you know how we liked her.' Later on the old man
had a go as well, in his ham-handed way, he said, 'Don't
let that girl go, Geoff, she's the best you've had.' I said,
'Jane? She's all right,' and he said in an embarrassed
voice, not looking at me, 'Seems very fond of you,' and it
leaped out, I said, 'Does she?'

When I left, they were quiet and looked unhappy. I
wished there was something I could give them, some hope,
some word. In the dark, at the gate, their faces were like
two sad moons.

CHAPTER TWELVE

On Monday, two things happened: Rosemary didn't come, and Jane phoned me.

Looking back, I've wondered what would have happened if it hadn't worked out like that; if Rosemary *had* turned up and Jane had phoned, or if she hadn't come, and Jane hadn't phoned, either. God knows.

Rosemary was due at three and I sat there waiting, half convinced she'd never come but still hoping; ten past three, twenty past, half past, hope going, phoning her, no reply, giving up; fuck her.

And then, at six o'clock, Jane. 'Geoff?' Very tentative, at first, but her voice was like a stab in the guts. I said, 'Yes?' She said, 'I'm still at Marion's.' I said, 'I see.' She said, 'It was nice of you to drive her over with the case.' I said, 'Any time,' ironically. There was a bit of a pause, then. She said, 'I'd like to see you.' I said, 'Would you? I'd like to see *you*. Come over.' She said, 'No, we've got to talk seriously. Let's have dinner in town.'

So we did, we ate at the Trattoria Firenze I'd always gone to with Audrey, perhaps because I wanted to exorcise her, I don't know. Jane said, 'Oh, it *is* nice, I've never been here before,' and I said, 'Yes, it is, isn't it?' a bit uneasy with all the waiters buzzing round and saying, 'Welcome back.' She gave me a look or two, but never said anything. In fact neither of us had much to say at all, we were struggling; where did you begin?

She looked tired and pale but still very pretty; it almost

suited her, the melancholy and the silence — silence always did. There was a sort of pathos about her now, especially when she smiled; sweet, but somehow resigned. I put my hand over hers on the table, and she smiled, then, I told her for the first time, 'I love you.' She said, 'Do you?' and her eyes shone, she was completely transformed and it made me feel uneasy, this power. I said, 'Yes. Yes, I do.' She said, 'Don't sound so surprised!' but I *was* surprised, it had slipped out, unpremeditated, though now I'd said it, I knew it was true. I said, 'You'll come back tonight, then?' She said, 'My things.' I said, 'We'll drive back for your things.' She said, 'It will be so late,' and I said, 'Oh hell, your things can wait until tomorrow, can't they?'

We sat there just smiling at each other, till she put on a voice and said, 'Anyway, there are things to talk about, first; you know there are.' I said, 'Okay, let's talk about them,' and she said, 'Not flippantly, like that; seriously!' I said, 'I've finished with Rosemary, if that's what you mean.' She said, 'And all the others?' I said, 'What others?' She said, 'The others you know now, the others that you're going to meet.' I said, 'Those, as well,' and she said, 'All right. I *will* come back.'

We didn't collect her cases, we went straight home and made love, because it needed that, we were both longing for it; pressing hands, touching each other's legs beneath the table. It was marvellous finding her body again, the lovely smoothness of her skin, the shape of her breasts. She kept saying, 'Oh, I love you, I love you!' and waking the next morning, feeling her warm beside me again, I was happy, somehow fulfilled, as if I'd reached the end of a journey.

I don't know when I said to her, 'Let's get married,' perhaps not at all. It was something we both assumed, a part of her coming back; maybe I asked her that night, in

147

the middle of making love, maybe we just started mentioning the wedding.

It had to be in church, to please her parents, which didn't really worry me, although it seemed ridiculous; the bullshit and the dressing-up and speeches. Besides, we were both of us agnostics, as far as you could put a label on it. It was fixed up at a church in Kensington where her parents went, when they remembered to; a place that went in for okay weddings, which made them happy, even if ours wasn't one.

They had to meet my parents, of course; something that had always made me laugh when I'd ever thought about it, but now just seemed an ordeal. We got them together at the flat, on neutral ground, for tea one Saturday, so it needn't last too long; and they sat there at first like dog and cat, not a word, sizing each other up, retiring, disapproving. I could almost hear Jane's mother say, who *are* these strange people? while mine was paralysed, poor thing, and I didn't blame her, with Mrs Ridding dressed to kill, mink coat, Harrod's suit, big diamond brooch above her big, left tit. Jane twittered away across the silences, but it was hard work.

I hadn't seen her father since the club; at the door he'd looked away from me and said, 'Congratulations,' as if it was a dirty word; and she said, 'Yes, Geoff, congratulations,' in an amazed, whoever-would-have-believed-it? voice; it was only the white wedding that had brought the two of them round.

In the end it was business that broke the deadlock. Ridding asked my father, 'You're a builder, aren't you?' and Dad said, 'Yes, that's right,' in a want-to-make-something-out-of-it? voice. But Ridding said, 'Having much effect on you, this new credit squeeze?' and they were away; he couldn't have done better if he'd asked how the chub were nibbling.

My father said, 'Having much effect? *I* should say it's having an effect,' and off they went together; the Government this and the Ministry of Housing that; the mortgage rates and the building societies and the insurance companies, on from there to the Trade Unions and the idle working man ('Bricklayers pulling down twenty-five quid a week I wouldn't have employed before the war; and can't touch them, can't *tell* them anything') till they were really swinging.

That gave us enough juice to get through the afternoon, though Mother was still scared stiff, poor thing, hardly opening her mouth, and when Mrs Ridding talked to her she patronised her — 'What do *you* think, Mrs Barnes?' — which annoyed me, although I'd quite expected it.

Jane had made a cake for tea, which was something else to talk about ('It's lovely, isn't it?' 'Yes, Jane does everything well') till at about six o'clock Mother whispered in Dad's ear and he made a great production out of looking at his watch, then saying, 'Well, we ought to be going.' The Riddings went, too, thank God, and that was all they saw of one another, till the wedding.

That wedding. It was a farce; or rather, a farce you stepped into under-rehearsed, with only your own lines and your own cues, when everybody else was word perfect in the whole play; mouthing your part, going through the motions and the gestures, none of it making sense, but the show just going on, in any case.

Because we had the works, the whole lot; morning coats and Ascot bloody toppers, organ music, speeches, even bridesmaids and pageboys; my brother's snotty-nosed kids, and her brother's. All the way down that aisle I was thinking, Jesus, Jesus, feeling ridiculous in those stupid clothes, knowing I looked like a coalheaver in a dinner jacket and that all those Establishment faces in the pews could see it; all her parents' friends, the stockbrokers and the colonels and the hunt ball ladies. You had to admit that he was going down with the flag flying.

Jane looked fine in her veil, like a madonna, very grave, a bit tearful — the proper white-wedding face, saying good-bye to her virginity. *She* enjoyed it, I could tell, though maybe it wasn't so much the ceremony as what the ceremony meant; she was home, this was it, we were married.

And John smiled through it, too, surprising me. He was best man — who else could I ask? — and the outfit suited him, *he* looked good in a top hat, quite aristocratic, and his manner was just right; the dryness, the handling everything with tongs.

We went back to Chiswick for the wedding breakfast — buffet — and when John spoke, he enjoyed himself, full of undertones, most of which I'm sure missed everyone but me, though now and again the hunt ball people would point suspiciously — like foxhounds picking up a scent.

John said it was marvellous to see people settle down, especially when they'd seemed the kind who wouldn't; that marriages were said to be made in Heaven, but they had to be *lived* on earth, and when he first knew me, he couldn't honestly imagine me living with anyone, or anyone with me, for more than a week or so. But then, again, one must never underestimate the love of a good woman, and here we all were to prove it. He didn't know Jane as well as he knew me, of course, but he was sure she *was* a good woman, besides being a very attractive one; one had only to look at the change in *me*.

When he said that I glanced at Jane, but she was smiling, smiling at everything. Her father spoke, waffling away, trying not to wince when he mentioned me. Mine had to speak too, poor devil, lumbering through a few sentences, sure we were all very appreciative, lucky to have such a lovely girl for a daughter-in-law, lucky this, lucky that, then I was on, God help me.

I stood there facing them, it was harder than acting; no darkened auditorium, you could see every bloody face you looked at, looking back at you: Jane in raptures, John amused, my parents proud, hers stiff-upper-lip, the Establishment people boring holes through me. But I'd worked at my speech and I spoke it like a zombie, no jokes—I could see how those faces would freeze. Just that I was grateful—very felicitous—grateful to them all for coming, grateful to my parents for everything they'd done for me, grateful to Jane's parents for allowing me to marry her, and to Jane for marrying me. Applause. God, how bloody grateful I was. Sitting down, I glanced at John, still smiling his pussy cat's smile, and I jumped up again. One joke. 'And, of course, for civilising me.' Laughter, like cracks in the rock.

We had a honeymoon, too; why not? Everything correct and proper and her parents were paying; weren't we entitled to the perks? We went to Nice; how conventional could you get? But it was nice with the sun out and the season just ending, not too crowded; swimming, lazing on the beach, hiring a car and scudding up into the cool hills among those trees, those marvellous mountains. And Jane was great, she was changed, it was remarkable. I'd never thought I'd so enjoy being somewhere alone with her.

What struck me most of all was how calm she was; no more do you love me? no more of those demands in almost everything she said or did or didn't say. Even the play was mentioned only once, and then as if she felt she owed it to me. I said, 'Shut up. No play. This is our honeymoon.' I was face down on the beach then and I couldn't see her, she was sitting above me in a deckchair, under a beach umbrella, but she ran her sandy toe down my back; the sort of thing she'd never have done before. But this was happening, too, this new playfulness, as if she'd somehow been released.

And I suppose she had; released from Mummy, released from Daddy, released from their voices on the telephone, the endless fear of what they'd say.

I bought a ridiculous, jazzy shirt, four different colours, and beach shorts and a yellow straw hat with a blue band. She wore a straw hat, too; a floppy, wide one, that was perfect for her. Very elegant she looked in the sunshine, with her hat and her dark glasses and her long white legs; never browning, keeping clear of the sun, afraid for her skin. I told her, 'You're like some gorgeous invalid.' She said, 'I burn. You wouldn't want me to burn, would you?' and I said, 'So what? We all burn, eventually.'

It was the life I loved; quite sensual; boozing, sunbathing and making love. I'd have been quite happy as a beach bum, looking back on a great future. I said once, 'Why can't we just stay here?'

We'd got out of the car in a tiny village in the hills; there were stalls and booths set up in the square and a primitive sort of band playing and dancing on the veranda of the little town hall.

Jane sighed and said, 'It would be nice, wouldn't it?' but I really meant it; why go back: to the rat race and the pressures and the bloody demands. I said, 'Shall we dance?' and we did, we bought tickets at the steps to the veranda, and went up. The floor was all bumpy, and I danced a very formal waltz with her, sending it up, full of flourishes, till everyone was watching and laughing. When we stopped and stood watching, ourselves, a good-looking young bloke with sideboards came up and bowed to us, then asked Jane to dance. I said, 'Go on, then, dance with him,' then danced myself with a little, dark dolly who smiled all the time and couldn't understand a word I said.

We must have been up there a couple of hours, dancing with each other, dancing with other people, and when it came out we were on our honeymoon, they cheered and brought out wine and made us drink with them, toasting us. I was half pissed by the time we drove back through the hills, singing, *Auprès de Ma Blonde* and just managing to dodge the oncoming traffic, with Jane beside me, saying, 'Careful, darling, careful!' and, 'I wish you wouldn't sing about a *blonde*,' half serious.

Down below, we suddenly saw the lights of the town, the yellow snake crawling round the waterfront, and beyond it, the lights of ships at sea. I said again, 'Why go back to London?' and she said in a religious sort of voice, 'But we must.'

And that night, it was back to reality; or a caricature of reality, as much of it as Hal Kaplan stood for; like the rat race run by Micky Mouse.

He didn't phone himself, thank God, it was John—'Hallo, are you enjoying yourselves?'—very cool. He said Hal had telephoned him six times that day, and he was nearly going mad. He'd said, 'Those contracts; I've got this deal'—he wouldn't say *what* deal—'I can't do anything until they're signed. What's the matter with Geoff? Why hasn't he called me? He hasn't called me in weeks. Is he angry because I didn't send a wedding present? He never even told me he was getting married. Listen; it was me who told him to; I told him, *marry* her!' I could just hear him.

John had told him that he didn't know where we were; somewhere on the Côte d'Azur, driving around. He said, 'He asked, would *I* sign, anyway, and I said not without you, and oughtn't he to talk to Anstruther, and he said agents were useless, they just screwed everything up, then on and on about integrity and all the work he'd put in and wanting to get home to see his children.' I said, 'Fend him off. You don't mind, do you?' and he said, 'Well, I'll *try*,' and obviously did mind, but I left him to it; I couldn't take the thought of Hal phoning five times a day all the rest of the honeymoon. As for the deal, I never even thought about it. Hal had never seemed quite real at any time, and even less so, now, living it up in the sun (courtesy of Jane's parents), staying in the big hotel on the sea front among all the people with expensive suntans, who looked as if they'd nothing else to think about in life; you had the suntan-lotion smell, here; it was the equivalent of the toilet-water smell, and I loved it.

I loved breakfast in bed, and Campari sodas and gin fizzes in the bar, and eating out on the terraces with the waiters gliding in and out making polite noises. Nothing mattered, money least of all, because we were living now as if we'd got it. 'We couldn't live *here*, Geoff,' she said, as if I didn't know that, but I'd still have stayed for the sun, wherever we lived; who cared?

A letter came from her mother—reality again—and she showed it to me, a paragraph that said ever so discreetly that if I was a good boy, Daddy might take me into partnership. I laughed when I saw that, I said, 'I'll open a Nice branch.' Me a bloody stockbroker, commuting, with striped pants and a comic bowler hat. Jane said, 'He means it well, darling,' all anxious, and I said, 'Yes, I suppose he does, poor old sod,' though I knew he'd shit himself if I accepted, having to face me day after day for the rest of his life; in his office, in his club. I bet it was his wife who put him up to it. Jane said, 'You can't expect him to understand you, Geoff.' I said, 'No, that's your prerogative,' and kissed her hand, because I hadn't meant it nastily. And she laughed, after a moment, where before she would have sulked.

So we went back—flew back, of course—and there was a cold drizzle falling as we came down the steps on to the tarmac. She shivered and linked her arm through mine, squeezing me tight as if to ask, it will still be the same, won't it?

154

But of course it couldn't be the same without the sun, without the sea, without the peace from the telephone, her parents, our 'responsibilities'. We hadn't been in the flat ten minutes when the phone rang, her mother, 'Welcome back,' and after that she was on every day, clucking over her; first, how was the honeymoon, was the hotel nice, was the sea warm; then, we must come and look at this flat she'd found. I said, 'She'll go on and on like this, if you let her.' Jane said, 'No, she won't; it's just that we're back, that's all,' and in fact, listening to her, I did seem to catch a different tone when she talked, you didn't get the same feeling of her being pushed up hard against a wall; at times she almost seemed to be humouring the old girl.

There was a lot of jazz about our moving, that the flat wasn't big enough — by which they meant it wasn't good enough — and the ones her mother found were always around Chiswick or Richmond or Kew, of course: I told Jane, no, thank you. Naturally, they'd 'help', that was made tactfully clear, and I had to admit that they'd been pretty generous, settling five thousand quid on her right away, giving us presents all the time, 'We thought you needed this.' Jane was afraid I might resent it, but why should I? If they wanted to, let them; they were presents to her, not me.

Hal Kaplan had disappeared, thank God, vanished in a puff of smoke, apparently, and a million telephone calls. John said that by the end he'd been practically tearful; how could we do this to him when he'd worked so hard for us, didn't we realise that he had a family he wanted to get back to? Then silence, peace. John said, 'Honestly, it's been like a holiday. Then this man rang up from the something or other syndicate, another American who knew about us from Kaplan; I put him on to Anstruther,' and I thought no more about it.

After about a week, we had John over for dinner, and it

was rather strained. Jane hadn't talked about him much, on the honeymoon, and when I'd mentioned him she'd been noncommittal; I wondered whether more of that speech had got across to her than I'd thought, at the time.

When I'd said, 'Let's have him over,' she'd said, 'All right, darling,' in an anything-to-make-you-happy voice, but she went to quite a lot of trouble with the dinner; hock and avocado pears and duckling and the napkins and tablecloth her parents had given her, the cutlery that had come from mine, all very gracious; a look at us, we're married, meal. John looked at it, and dug it right away. She was wearing a new dress, too, one she'd bought herself with a cheque some uncle gave us for the wedding, red chiffon, very elegant; she and John met like two great hostesses at the same party; 'Don't you look *spe*cial, Jane?' 'Do you think so, John?' not a flicker of a smile, and that set the pattern for the evening. We were back to the beginning, they were cat and dog again, or rather, cat and cat, both of them watchful and touchy, talking to each other as little as possible, raising subjects that excluded the other, though every now and then John would throw her a compliment, '*Lovely* avocado pears, *gorgeous* duckling,' and she'd say, 'Thank you,' deadpan, mopping them up like blotting paper.

What John seemed to need, I couldn't help feeling, was something from *me*; he kept glancing at me in a worried, expectant way and I suppose, looking back, that what he wanted was reassurance, and I couldn't give it him, I couldn't join in against her. Did I still need him? he seemed to be asking. Did I still want to have him around? It was almost as if he felt he'd lost a war and had come to find out the peace terms. Jane did say when he went, 'You know you're always welcome, John,' but it was gracious lady stuff, what mattered was that she *could* say it to him at all, and the poor sod looked miserable, then pulled himself together and said, '*Thank* you,' very ironic, even with a little bow.

Then there was the new flat. 'I wonder if we *should* move, Geoff, it *is* a bit cramped,' the party line. I said, 'Not really. You're hardly here in the day.' She said, 'If we have children … ' which was about the only time she'd ever brought it up, and I said, 'Okay, if we do, we'll move, but we aren't, are we?'

I weakened in the end, though. She started looking, herself, and she found a place in Palace Gardens Terrace, the other side of the Park, four rooms and seven pounds a week, unfurnished. Showing me round, she behaved as if she was trying to sell me the place; wasn't this lovely, wasn't that marvellous? Wasn't it beautifully quiet, although it was so central? Didn't I like the long, deep bath in the bathroom? Couldn't we do some lovely things with the main room if we took down all this dreary wallpaper and painted the walls white? And I thought how strange it was that since the wedding she'd been behaving exactly like a bride, down to everything except the bridal night; she might never have been living with me. It was almost as if she'd been reborn.

And the new flat seemed the climax of it all, without which things couldn't be complete. Now she'd latched on to it, now I'd given way, there was no holding her; carpets, curtains, furniture, wallpaper. We painted the living-room ourselves, she was surprisingly good at that sort of thing — with rollers, wearing overalls, she looked fine in hers; paint on her face, and her hair falling over her forehead. I didn't mind; it gave me something to do, a feeling I was working. Her parents wanted *her* to give up work, that was one of the things behind the Stock Exchange offer; but she wouldn't, bless her, she said to me, 'It wouldn't be fair, I'd have married you under false pretences. If I stopped working now it would make us too dependent on them;

157

and you've got to have time for your work.' My work.

It was early in the New Year when we moved, a hellish day with the rain coming down in that sullen way that means it's set for twenty-four hours. The removal men came blundering in like they always do, desecrating things and dropping them, chipping paintwork, knocking corners, and as I watched them, I had an odd feeling in my stomach. Something was ending. I'd let go of something; now, I'd be adrift.

Not her, though. Driving to the flat through the rain, behind the great, square, hideous removal van, she rested her head on my shoulder, gave one of her sighs, and said, 'Aren't you happy, Geoff?' I said, 'Me? Yes, of course.' She said, '*Really* happy?' and I said, 'Look, honey, we've moved, that's all there is to it. It's a nice flat, I like it, I'm happy; okay?' But she was quiet the rest of the way, and it was only when we got into the place that she perked up again.

For those first few weeks, she played dolls' houses with it, let's put this here, wouldn't that be better there; deliveries arriving all the time — 'Do you like *this*? I got it in the Portobello Road?'

She was in the Portobello Road every Saturday morning, and sometimes she dragged me with her, in and out of the barrows, in and out of the antique shops, always so excited — 'Look at *this*, Geoff!' — like a child, with the barrow boys acting it up like mad, playing characters — 'Yes, lady, you won't do no better than that' — like some Hollywood film on London. And the debby birds drifting through, all elegant and very languid — 'Isn't it di*vine*?' — doing a bit of genteel slumming.

Some of my furniture stayed in the flat; most of it went, before long. I didn't argue much, I couldn't really blame her; a lot of it was tat. It was a funny feeling when the sofa went, though; they seemed to be carrying out my past, all the birds who'd sat on it and cried on it and been seduced on it. A few things stayed; my roll top desk, an armchair, a couple of hardbacked chairs, shoved into the smallest room of the lot; my den. Except, of course, that I worked in the living-room.

Outside, it was another world from Earl's Court; the faces you saw, the voices you heard; more settled, much more bourgeois, lots of prams and nannies, though Notting Hill Gate wasn't so different, bar the skyscrapers; lots of little dollies and a lot of spades — which was something new.

Jane still couldn't do too much for me; she still kept buying little presents, consolation prizes; gloves, a scarf, new slippers.

After we'd been in about three weeks, she brought up the play, again: 'I don't want to nag you, darling, but it's so good, you *ought* to finish it.' So I started going through the motions, trying to get up a head of steam, again, just not managing it, though whenever I read it to her it was always, 'Marvellous, Geoff,' peals of laughter, falling about, 'Darling, you've *got* to go on!'

John was round once and he saw it lying on a chair, and smiled, 'The play?' and I picked it up and shoved it in a drawer. He said, 'You *must* let me see it, some time,' and I said, 'It's crap.' He smiled again, into my face, as if to say he knew it was, and he knew why I was writing it. I felt like getting it out again and ripping it to shreds; 'Oh, Geoff, how *could* you?' (we'd already had that over the ornaments, how could I?) but I knew that would amuse him all the more. Perhaps that's what he wanted me to do.

About a week after that he rang me, and I'd never heard him so excited. He said, 'The syndicate was real! They've made an offer!' I said, 'What syndicate? What offer?' and he said, 'The ones who rang when you were in France. A features syndicate. That was why Kaplan kept phoning! He knew they wanted it.' I said, 'Wanted *what*?'

159

but I was getting steamed up, too; there was obviously something happening. He said, 'The strip cartoon rights! Syndication! Ninety pounds a week! For *The Inquisitive Camel*!' and I said, *'What?* Say that again!' and he did, he gradually calmed down and explained.

There was an American agency, Rex Features Syndicate, that handled strip cartoons; they'd a London office, and their American boss was in town. John said, 'Hal told him he owned the rights; no wonder he wanted us to sign!' I shouted, 'Christ, come over! Let's get drunk!' then rang up Jane and told her, 'Ninety quid, that's forty-five pounds a week!'

She said, 'Geoff, that's wonderful!' all breathless, 'but are you sure?' I said, 'Positive! They've made the offer! Listen, let's all meet for lunch!' it was on the spur of the moment, but she said, 'I don't think I can, darling, we're so busy, today,' and I got the message; why the hell couldn't anything be easy and straightforward? I said, 'Anyway: you're pleased.' She said, 'Of course I'm pleased.'

That depressed me until John got round, but when he did the news was too damn good to go on feeling down, and I thought perhaps it was just as well, we didn't want a spectre-at-the-feast touch, undertones, me being torn in half again, between them. I wanted just to celebrate and enjoy it, this bloody ridiculous thing from out of the skies, and if it turned out not to be true, we'd have had the celebration.

So I said, 'Let's make it the Ivy.' John said, 'Good God, can we afford it?' I said, 'Of course not, but we will be able to. Charge it up against the first ninety quid.' I'd been there only once in my life when my play was running in the West End (running ...) with a producer who had some Anglo-Yugoslav cowboy film lined up, that never came to anything.

The place had that toilet-water touch again, you could just feel all the money in the air. The panelling and the maroon banquettes, the green, leaded window panes, keeping out the peasants.

John was sitting at a table in the bar with a gin-and-tonic, as though he was afraid they'd turn him out at any moment; when he saw me he looked terribly relieved. I ordered two more doubles right away, and by the time our table was ready, we were both a little high.

When the wine waiter came, I said, 'Champagne!' John raised his eyebrows at me, but I said, 'Jesus Christ, what else?' So we drank champagne and got more pissed, and the higher John got the camper he got, I'd never seen him sloshed before. I put on our Hal Kaplan voice and said, 'There's just one thing, John. There has to be a romantic interest. We can't sell the camel in the States without a romantic interest, even if it has to be a dromedary,' and John said, 'What romantic interest could there *poss*ibly be, except the Sphinx?' I said, 'Blocked by the sands of the Nile,' and he said, 'Precisely. We could call it "The Hump on the Camel".' I said, 'Great. That fits in with all the other famous strip cartoons, Lil Abner and the rest. The hero never gets the girl.'

We staggered out of the Ivy giggling, then back to my place, and by the time Jane got in, we were on whisky, and still pretty paralytic. As soon as he heard her key, John shot out of his chair saying, 'Oh, God, I ought to go; she'll say I've been corrupting you!' I said, 'Stay, stay!' then Jane came in and did a double-take; before we could speak, I told her, 'We've been celebrating.' She said, 'So I see.' I said, 'You should have been with us.' She said, 'How could I?' and went out into the bedroom, mother figure; I'll leave you children to play.

John said, 'I *must* go,' and I said, 'Oh, Christ,' and I got out of my chair, but now I felt different from before, it

161

wasn't the old thing, standing up to her, resenting her; I wanted them to *like* each other. So I poured out another whisky and followed her into the bedroom. I said, 'Here you are. Have a drink. Wet the camel's head.' She gave me a quick glance and said, 'No, thank you.' I said, 'Come on! You're spoiling the party!' She said, 'I just don't feel like one,' and I said, 'Aren't you glad?' She said, 'Of *course* I'm glad!' and I sent her up, I said, 'Of course I'm glad! You bloody sound it!' and she said, 'Do I have to get drunk to prove I'm glad?' I said, 'Oh, Christ, you sound like the bloody Salvation Army. It's forty-five pounds a week, haven't you got that into your head?' and she turned on me, she shouted, 'Yes, it's marvellous, it's wonderful, I'm delighted! *Now* are you satisfied?' and I shouted back at her, 'No, I'm not! It's all because of John, isn't it? If it had happened to the play, you'd be dancing round the room!'

At that moment, we heard the front door shut, and we were both quiet, facing each other, looking at each other, not moving. Then she said, 'I'll go and call him back, if you like,' and she went, quickly, too, hurrying to the front door; I heard her calling, 'John! John!' then opening it, and running down the stairs. It was five minutes before she got back, out of breath; she said, 'I couldn't catch up with him, I called after him, I followed him right the way up to Notting Hill Gate; but the faster I went, the faster *he* went. In the end, he got into a taxi.' I said, 'Never mind,' and put my arm round her shoulders. I felt horribly sober now, and miserable. She said, 'I did try.' I said, 'I know you did.' She said, 'I *am* glad,' and I said, 'I know, I know.'

I pulled her down on the bed, and we made love.

CHAPTER THIRTEEN

Later that week, we met the Rex Features boss, Joe Crawley; he took us to lunch, with Anstruther, at the Caprice, the money smell, again; more hectic and hysterical this time, pink and flouncy, with the tables jammed close together and everybody talking loud.

Not Crawley, though; he was one of those big, quiet, smooth *sincere* men, who *listened* to you — this is me, listening — and obviously came to England for his suits (double-breasted blue pinstripe). He *believed* in the camel, he thought the whole idea was something new and he was always looking for something new, he'd been real surprised when Mike Anstruther here told him Hal Kaplan didn't own the rights, like he'd said.

Anstruther was young and very hip, full of gossip — London gossip, New York gossip, Hollywood gossip — good-looking, in a way that made you think he must spend three hours a week at the barber's. He seemed to know how to jolly Crawley along, rather like an Indian boy with an elephant. We agreed to let Crawley have half-a-dozen four-panel strips before he went back to the States, which was in ten days, and he said, 'Would you? Would you really? That would be wonderful!' sincere as all get-out, then told us he could guarantee us between a dozen and twenty outlets for a start, then take it from there; some of their strips sold to two or three hundred papers.

We staggered out, slightly pissed, again, half excited by this picture of what we could make if things went well, half terrified in case he'd think the specimens were crap when we'd done them, though Anstruther told us not to worry, it was a formality, Crawley was sold on it; he even rang that afternoon to say, 'Those two charming young people.' Anstruther said, 'I've told him there's competition, he'll be lucky if he gets you.'

But we were still worried about it. We worked for hours at a stretch, right into the night at John's place, though at mine he'd start looking at his watch round five o'clock, and scooting out of the door soon afterwards. I dreamed up a new story line that had the camel mixed up with the Foreign Legion, we finished the half-dozen strips within a week and drove them over reverently to Anstruther, in Shoe Lane, then we sat tight and sweated it out. Jane said, 'I'm *sure* they'll take it, darling,' in her *soothing* voice, the one that drove me mad. She'd raved about how clever the story was, how terribly inventive, till I got a bit tired of it and said, 'The drawings are good, too'—they were—and she said, 'Yes, they *are* good, darling, but they're not as original as the text.'

Crawley flew back without giving a decision and we thought, that's it, I went into a terrible depression, I told Jane, '*I* know, you don't *want* the thing to go,' and she cried, and I apologised. But a few days later, Anstruther got a cable, it was okay, he read it to me over the phone; eight newspapers in the States had said yes, France, Italy and Germany were all interested; he was advancing us fifteen hundred dollars.

Jesus, it was a great feeling to be going around again with money in your pocket, money that you'd earned, yourself. The work was good, too, not like bloody advertising—and the best thing about it was that we weren't working in the dark any more, every minute was paid for.

I went out and bought Jane a ring, one of those antique, cameo rings she went in for, I *felt* like giving her something, after all the things she'd given me. When I did, it seemed to overwhelm her, she stood there holding the package with tears in her eyes, it made me feel ashamed, I said, 'Open it!' and after a second, she did. When she got the ring out of its box, she said, 'Geoff!' again, staring and staring at it, and I said, 'Like it?' because all this gratitude was just too much, it was killing me. She said, 'It's lovely.' I said, 'Put it on, then,' and she said, 'No, *you* put it on for me,' and I did, it was like a little ceremony.

When I'd done it, she flung her arms round my neck and nuzzled into my shoulder, not speaking, and I had this funny mixture of feelings, cancelling each other out: guilt and irritation and pleasure because she liked it. Next day, she bought me a gold tie-clip. I could never stay ahead.

We had a house-warming for the new flat; her parents, my parents (I caved in), John and a few of our friends who'd be certain to behave themselves. One of them was Dave, I'd nearly asked him to the wedding, except that knowing how grotesque the whole damn thing would be, I hadn't, I wanted to get through it without observers, and Dave was an observer.

I noticed it again as he wandered round the flat, looking at the books, the pictures on the walls—reproductions, mostly, except for one or two of John's; the old tat. Cézanne and Van Gogh and the Chinese Girl, to make Jane feel at home. On the phone, I'd told him about the camel strip, and he'd roared with laughter, he'd said, 'That's terrific! No, don't be surprised; this is how it happens. One day, nothing, the next day, you're buying yourself a Cadillac. That's show business!' and it was good in a way to hear him taking it for granted, it made it seem more real, not just a bubble that would burst at any minute. At the same time, it didn't seem as comical to me as it did to him; forty-five quid a week was no joke.

Now, at the party, Dave said, 'Let's see it! Where's the

165

camel?' and I took him into the study, where I had a few roughs of strips that we'd done.

He picked them up and laughed his head off, he said, 'That's great, that's really great! *The Desert Song* on paper! It'll run for years!' then John came in to see what the laughing was about, and Dave said, 'Sigmund Romberg, I presume! Congratulations! I wish your camel long life! It's the greatest thing since Bambi!' and he went out of the room still laughing, while John and I looked at one another, and John shrugged. What was so funny?

One thing I noticed at the party: a change in Jane's parents; she'd told them, and she must have rubbed it in. They hadn't quite come round to me, yet, but now there was a sort of restraint in her father's attitude, almost respect—not for me, so much, as for money. He had to bring it up, eventually: 'I hear you and your friend are doing awfully well with those drawings of yours.' I said, 'Not too badly,' and he said in a puzzled way, 'Splendid, splendid. It's not the sort of thing I really understand much about.' I said, 'Neither do we,' and left him to it.

As for her, there she was doing her dowager act, wearing a sleeveless dress; big, white, rubber arms: 'Congratulations, Geoff,' and I had this impression I'd had the first time I'd met her, that she really went for me, and that now she could show it again: I wasn't a bum any more.

My poor mother and father holed up in a corner, inevitably, but Jane was nice to them and so was John, and old Ridding huffed and puffed to the old man about stocks and shares. My mother said to me, 'You're looking so much *better*, darling.' I said, 'More money!' and she said, 'No, not just *that*; more relaxed, and everything.' I said, 'Of course. Just like you told me I would,' and she said, 'Get away with you!'

But the fact was I did feel better, and I suppose this was probably one of the happiest times in my life; getting on with Jane, money coming in, doing work I enjoyed. I sold the M.G. and bought a new Triumph on hire purchase; we were both making sixty quid a week by now, and in England, the *Daily News* bought the strip. It was great to see it every morning with our names there, Hendren and Barnes—like two cross-talk comedians, I told John. But it did mean something to me, it was proving something, just like it did when I was acting and I used to look at my name on the bills, there it was; something you could *see*.

And there was quite a lot you could do with the strip, the old social comment bit—not too obvious, otherwise they'd sling it out—sending up things like colonialism and snobbery and De Gaulle. John said he'd even read an article somewhere about the comic strip as a new art form, but when I asked Dave did he know anything about it, he did his laughing act again, I was getting rather tired of it. He said, 'All this and significance *too*?' but why the hell not?

The camel book was published and got some very nice reviews; it didn't sell badly, either. Another thing was that I got going on the play, as if having recognition for one thing unblocked me for the other. The whole idea seemed funny again, and I finished the second act and got busy on the third. Jane was ecstatic.

What had happened, I imagine—if you analyse it—was that I'd found a new rhythm, there was a pattern in my life for the first time since I'd given up the theatre. I could look back, now, and see that the years between giving up and marrying Jane had been a sort of interval, where I was looking for things; for what I was, if I wasn't an actor, for who I wanted to live with. They'd been bad years, really, destructive years and self-destructive years; the baby, Audrey. I could see, now, why I'd gone for a girl like Audrey—she was the perfect symbol of them—why I'd rejected one like Jane. But she hadn't given up, thank God.

I once told her, 'Jesus, I was nasty to you,' and she said,

'But it was only part of you, the surface part; I knew there was so much more underneath.' I said, 'I owe you a lot.'

One night, lying beside her in the dark—it had to be in the dark—I even told her about the baby. She was quiet for a long time, till I began to feel worried, then at last she said, 'You poor thing.' I said, 'Me? Poor thing?' She said, 'Yes. To be blackmailed like that. It was blackmail.' I said, 'But I walked out on them. I ran away,' and Jane said, 'She didn't *have* to have it. She wanted to punish you.' I said, 'But it's alive. It's my son. I ought to see him,' and she said, 'What good would it do? You'd upset him and you'd upset yourself. Leave him alone. There's nothing you can do for him.' And I saw that she was right, what *could* I do for him? I had this great feeling of release, I felt more grateful to her than ever.

She still didn't talk about *our* having children, and God knows *I* never brought it up, I'd had enough, it was something that I couldn't even think about. When my mother hinted at it I'd change the subject; once, I even snarled at her, I said, 'What's the *hurry*? You've got two grandchildren already, haven't you?' and she blinked and said, 'No hurry, darling, but there's no harm wanting more, is there? Anyway, it's natural.' I knew she'd got at Jane, as well, saying, 'You do *want* children, dear?' and Jane said, 'I told her, my first responsibility was to *you*.'

Now, we went over to them once a month, and once a month they came to us. We worked out an arrangement with Jane's parents, too; I said, 'Otherwise, they'll overrun us, especially your mother,' dinner with them once a fortnight, boring as all hell, them to us every four weeks. Her mother was for ever wanting to come over for this, drop in for that, and I took to being out when she did; those were my evenings for working with John, till Jane began to take a firmer line with her, 'No, Mummy, it's *not* convenient.'

John was the only real problem; he and Jane still just suffered one another, though they both realised it was a losing battle; I was married to Jane, I was working with John.

The trouble was that now we were working so much more closely, our differences were becoming more obvious. We hadn't got the same point of view, the same sense of humour; John had this cosy-camp thing, I wanted to be bolder. I talked about it to Jane, and she said, 'It's what I've always told you, darling; John is *much* more conventional than you are.' I said, 'What do you want? I can't just ditch him,' and she said, 'No, of course; you're very loyal.'

He and I disagreed a lot over the camel strips, though it never boiled up into a real argument; John's way of disagreeing was usually to go very quiet and sullen, carrying on under protest. At the same time, the strip itself couldn't have been going better, we had twenty outlets, now, and Anstruther thought that in a year we might have fifty.

What did bring the explosion, funnily enough, wasn't the camel but the play. I finished it one afternoon in the middle of May, rang up Jane right away to tell her, read it to her when she got home, then took her out to dinner. Next morning, at his flat, I told John about it, I felt really good, I said, 'I've finished the play!' and he said, 'Good!' without as much as looking at me. I said, 'Well, for Christ's sake, you might sound pleased.' He said, 'Of course I'm pleased, but after all, it is such a *private* thing, isn't it?'

I said, 'No, it's not. One of these days, I hope it'll be performed.' He said, 'I hope so, too.' I said, 'You sound as if you do.' He said, 'How can you ex*pect* me to sound, when you haven't even let me read it?' and the penny dropped, I said, 'Okay, okay, I'll let you read it,' and he said, 'You're sure *Jane* wouldn't mind?'

For a moment I was pulled up short, then I said, 'You bloody sod.' He said, 'Call me whatever you like; you know I'm right, she *would* mind. The play's like her baby.'

I said, 'Right, there's nothing more to say, then, is there?' and started going out. As I reached the front door I heard him say, 'The play ... or you,' and I slammed it hard.

That evening, just as I was telling Jane about it, he rang and apologised. He said, 'I didn't mean it. I was upset about something else,' so we patched it over, but it wasn't the sort of thing that you forget. Jane said, 'It's what I've always thought, darling; he's jealous of you, he's jealous of me because of you; you *mustn't* let him hold you back.' I said, 'Yes, yes, yes, I know,' but it had upset me.

I was partly to blame, perhaps; I may have talked like that about the play to him at one time, but now it was different, now it was *my* play, as well. I needed re-assurance on it, and I gave it to Dave to read, which was a mistake, I should have remembered how he laughed at the camel, but who *could* I ask? I wasn't ready to submit it, and I still didn't like the sound of Jane's theatre critic; whenever I looked at his notices, he was always tearing something to shreds.

Dave said, 'A play? Really? Sure, I'll read it.' A week went by without a word from him, and I was getting anxious; the end of it was that I rang him up, myself.

He said, 'Hi! How's the camel? Still on tour? How did you make out in Rochdale?' I did my best to laugh, then to ask him what *he'd* been doing, and got a long moan about how he'd been trying to set up some documentary in Iceland, and at the last moment the programme heads had turned it down. From there he got on to what was wrong with television, and the longer he kept on, the more afraid I was to ask, it seemed to me he was deliberately sheering away from it. In the end, I just had to know, I asked him, 'Have you read my play?' He said, 'Your play? Sure,' and there was a pause, then I said, 'And?' He said, 'I'll talk to you about it. We'll discuss it, some time.' I said, 'What was your general impression?' He said, 'My *general* impression? My general impression was that maybe you'd do better sticking to the camel.'

Boomp, just like that, knocking all the wind out of me. I said, 'Okay. Thanks. I'll see you, then,' and put the phone down. It was what I'd really known all along, at least until these last few weeks. Of course it was crap, it always had been, it was Jane who'd talked me into it and made me finish it and left me open to slaps like this one I'd had. It sickened me.

I tried to talk myself out of it. I had the camel, hadn't I? At least the camel was swinging, going in six different countries, making more money all the time. But it didn't work; what the hell was a strip cartoon? 'I'm a playwright.' People respected that. 'As a matter of fact, I write a strip cartoon.' People heard that and they laughed, you couldn't blame them. 'How does one *write* a strip cartoon?' Very comical.

I was meant to work with John that afternoon, but I just didn't feel like it. I rang him up and said I'd got a cold, then I went to the Classic at Notting Hill Gate to see *Citizen Kane*. In a way, it was the last film to choose; I sat there watching Orson Welles and thinking Christ, he does everything well, he acts in it, he wrote it, he directed it, and look at *me*. I can just about manage half a strip cartoon.

When I got back, I felt more depressed than ever. Jane was there, and as soon as she saw me she said, 'What's the matter?' I said, 'Nothing,' I was choked with her. She said, 'There *is*, darling; what's gone wrong?' and I said, 'Just that I've at last had an ob*jec*tive reaction to my *great* play.' She bristled like a cat—*our* play, *our* kitten—she said, '*Whose* reaction?' I said, 'Dave's,' and she said with this same, angry look, 'What did he say?'

I said, 'He told me the truth, that's all. He told me I ought to stick to camels, and he's right.' She said, 'He's *not* right! How *dare* he? He's just jealous!' I said, 'Jealous! Everyone's jealous! Why the hell should he be jealous of me?' She said, 'Lots of reasons.' I said, 'Name *one*,' and she said, 'Because you're successful. Remember how he laughed about the camel.' I said, 'I don't blame him. Successful! What kind of success is that?' She said, 'And what about *him*? What has *he* done? Haven't you told me how he's always complaining to you?' and on and on until I thought, well, maybe she has got something, maybe I *should* show the play around a bit, but not yet, I didn't feel up to it, yet; and certainly not to her drama critic.

She said, 'Why don't you give it to an agent? He can submit it for you,' and I said, 'If I can find one who'll handle it.' Still, the idea wasn't bad. At least with an agent you didn't get the comebacks yourself.

So I sent it to an agent who kept it a month, then sent it back with a polite note, they were overloaded, and I said, 'Oh, for God's sake let's put it away and forget about it.' She said, 'No, give it to me, I've an idea.' I said, 'I know; your critic friend.' She said, 'At least he can give us some advice.' But all he said, or all she'd tell me he said, was that plays like this weren't being put on in the West End just now.

I put it away again, then, thinking about it, I realised he was right. At the moment it was all kitchen sink, or this new bit, all Cockney repartee that added up to something so profound not even the actors understood it. The end of it was that I began another play, only this time not a comedy. It was about Audrey, about this cool chick who gets married to a millionaire, then wishes she hadn't; very moral. It was a good theme, the only thing that worried me was that Jane might get upset about it; I told her when I started, 'Some of it's Audrey.' But she loved this one, too — 'in quite a different way' — she said it was a marvellous piece of observation.

CHAPTER FOURTEEN

It was early September; I was sitting downstairs in the Trattoria Firenze, waiting for John, when suddenly she walked down the stairs.

I saw her, and my stomach turned to water, I prayed she'd turn around and go straight back upstairs, I picked up the big menu card and held it in front of my face. But when I looked out again she was still there, beautiful and arrogant and suntanned, all the same old things, gazing round the restaurant in that supercilious way. She was wearing a pale blue turban that gave her an Etruscan look, and a light-blue tailored suit that was sure to have come from Paris. All at once, she turned her head and saw me, and her eyes lit up, she said, 'Geoff!'

I said, 'Hallo, Audrey.' She said, 'My God!' and came over to my table, giving me her cheek to kiss. I could hardly bring out any words, I mumbled something about surprises, about how well she looked, how actually I was waiting for John, and she said, 'Well, it's lucky you're here, you can buy me lunch.'

For a moment I was speechless, struggling for an excuse, wanting to say no—I never could, to her—but all that came out was, 'Okay,' and she sat down, smiling, very cool, she said, 'I had a half appointment with Giulio Cardoni, but he said he'd probably have to go to Rome to finish dubbing.' I simply looked at her, the rabbit and the snake, I'd got nothing to say, I just wished John would come, and she looked at *me*, her appraising look, she said,

'You're so much *fatter!*' I said, 'Am I?' She said, 'And sleeker and more prosperous; quite, quite different. But then you're a success, now, aren't you? It's funny, I could never imagine you being a success.' I said, 'Success!' She said, 'Of course you are; your strip cartoon. I read it every day. That marvellous camel.' And I felt stupidly pleased because she didn't sneer at it any more, she admired it.

She said, 'And you're married, aren't you? Why didn't you invite me to your wedding?' I just looked at her, still hypnotised. She said, 'To that girl; Joan.' I said, 'Jane.' She said, 'The faithful unto death one who was always giving you things.' I said, 'Yes.' She looked at me again and said, 'Your suit! And a button-down collar!' and while she talked, while she enjoyed herself, she made me feel ridiculous, like a turkey being fattened for Christmas, or a big, fat, doctored tom cat.

When John arrived I was delighted, though as soon as he saw her he looked as if he'd turn and run, she'd always frightened him. I said, 'John, it's Audrey; do you remember Audrey?' He gave a sort of frozen nod, and she said, 'Congratulations on your camel! You draw him, don't you?' and he said, 'Oh, well, thank you,' shooting a look at me, but it was enough to get him to sit down.

She asked us how it all happened, we imitated Hal Kaplan to her and she laughed at that, then she said to John, 'Don't you think Geoff's changed?' He said, 'Changed?' She said, 'Yes, since his marriage. Since he made it,' and I caught a sort of gleam in his eye, though all he said was, 'Yes, I suppose so,' and she said, 'You see him all the time, of course; I haven't seen him for God knows how long.'

Since then she seemed to have been everywhere; to Tahiti and Tangier and Corsica, to Cortina and Hollywood and Rome. And watching her, listening to her talk in that metallic voice, I felt things stirring in me which had been sleeping, things that I had but wasn't using. I realised my new play just hadn't got her, I hadn't got this power of hers, this electricity, this thing I still responded to and needed, when I'd thought that I was free.

At the same time, she could still upset me, she could still make me feel like a clown, and I'd lost the defences that I'd built against her. I wasn't used to being laughed at, any more.

She began to bring John into it, too; asking was I an attentive husband —'I could never see him as a husband' —had I become domesticated, and he said, 'Oh, yes, terribly domesticated,' just ironically enough to be ambiguous. She said, 'Yes, I can imagine that, just looking at him; like a pasha. Is he waited on hand and foot? Does she spoil him?' John said, 'Well, a little.' 'Does she mother him?' and he went po-faced as if to say it wasn't *his* business.

She said, 'She does, doesn't she? She does!' and I got angry, I said, 'All right, she does, what the hell does it matter?' She said, 'I'd love to see it. Will you invite me? When can I come round?' I said, 'Oh, some time,' and I saw John smile, very discreet, not meaning to be noticed, maddening me.

She dropped it, then, and started talking about the exhibitions she'd been to and the paintings she'd bought, mostly to John, it was *his* subject, and I left them to it, I was choked by now. She said she'd like to look at *his* work and he said he'd love her to, they were like conspirators, and it was Jane who'd brought them together, getting at Jane; he'd take any chance he got. I felt like walking out on them but couldn't, she still riveted me, even now she made me ache for her.

She turned to me and said, 'Don't sulk, we were only teasing you,' she put her hand on my arm, and I shrugged and swallowed, then I talked again; about people we

175

knew, like Dave. She said, 'Oh, Dave; he never *finishes* anything,' which gave me a new line on him, one I was almost pleased to have.

When the coffee came, John said he'd have to go and I thought, sod it, I'll go with him and to hell with her, there was this tug-of-war, go or stay, wanting to do both, to spite her and to stay with her, knowing if I left her I'd feel miserable, knowing what I risked if I didn't. And perhaps she sensed this, because she touched me again and said, 'You don't have to go, yet, do you?' and I found myself saying, 'No, not yet.'

So there we were, alone together, and she said, 'I'm sure he's in love with you.' I said, 'Oh, for Christ's sake, Audrey.' She said, 'He used to be jealous of me, now he's jealous of her.' I said, 'You still love stirring it up.' She said, 'But darling, it's perfectly obvious.' I said, 'Still dragging things into the light. What good does it do?' She said, 'More good than sweeping them under the carpet.'

She looked at me and smiled, and in that smile, that moment, I knew she wanted me; that as sure as hell we'd soon be in bed together, and I shook all over at the excitement of it, yet it frightened me, like stepping off a precipice.

She said, 'Well?' and I just shook my head. Under the table my leg touched hers, and I pushed up hard against her; she didn't move away. She asked, 'Are you happy?' and I thought, I *was* happy, I didn't look at her, I said, 'Yes, I suppose so. Are you?' She said, 'Oh, I'm up and down. Perhaps *I* ought to get married. You've encouraged me.' I said, 'Have I?'

She laughed and put her hand over mine, squeezing my fingers hard. I asked, 'What are you going to do, now?' She said, 'Nothing much. Why? Do you want to come back to tea?' I looked up at her and I said, 'Yes.' We held one another's eyes. Hers were amused, but at the same time sensual; the kind of look I'd forgotten, that I never had from Jane.

When she saw the Triumph she said, 'A success symbol?' She was driving a Mercedes, now; she drove as crazily as ever. Following her to Sloane Street I was thinking, why not, what's wrong with it, what's wrong if I need both of them?

In the lift we kissed, we came together automatically, and inside her flat we undressed each other right away, there beside the door. She said, 'Look at you!' and grabbed my stomach, 'Look at all this success!' then worked her hand inside my pants, on to my cock, and said, 'At least *that* hasn't changed!'

Making love with her was as good as ever, better; I'd forgotten how adventurous it could be, how you could lose yourself, up there on the roller coaster, soaring and plunging; how passionate she was, how possessed, biting, sucking, pinching, never passive, not even in the orgasm when she writhed and sighed as if she was on the rack, as if I'd taken her against her will.

And this time it was better afterwards, no bitterness, no sudden hatred, who are *you*? She lay there with this smile again, and said, 'Come to Paris!'

It was as though she'd stuck a knife in me. I said, 'Paris? When?' She said, 'This week-end.' I said, 'Christ, I wish I could.' She said, 'Why can't you? Won't she let you? Do you have to get permission?' I said, 'Jesus, Audrey.' She said, 'Come, then,' and swung off the bed, leaving me there, my head spinning, one moment thinking, of course I can't, the next, what harm can it do?

When she came back she asked, 'Decided?' I said, 'No,' and looked at her, and that decided for me; how she looked, so slim and brown, her eyes alight, her hair falling loose down to her shoulders; how could I bear to lose her?

She said, 'Is this the first time that you've been unfaithful?' I said, 'Yes,' and she said, 'Then I've robbed you of your virginity!' and she jumped on to the bed beside me, running her fingers down my chest, her tongue over my lips. She said, 'Never mind, it doesn't matter, I shan't disturb your domesticity.' I said, 'I'm coming,' and before she could answer, put my tongue in her mouth.

At home I thought, Christ, what had I done? I was back before Jane and I mooned around the flat, wondering how to tell her, whether to say that it was Paris or not, and if I did, how to get out of taking her, whether I shouldn't just forget the whole thing, and I was torn again. Why the hell had I agreed? Why the hell was life so complicated? Why the hell had I picked this day in that restaurant?

I'd said it to Audrey and she'd smiled, all knowing, and she'd said, 'It's obvious.' I said, 'Oh, yes. Because *you* go there. Because I wanted to see you. Christ, I must have been there a dozen times.' She said, 'But this time I was there!'

When Jane did come in, I found her irritating me; her voice, the things she asked, the need to lie to her. It was as though seeing Audrey put the clock back, so that all the things I'd learned to live with needled me again. Jesus, I thought, how stupid she is, and Jesus, how she fusses.

I said, 'Look, I may have to go to Paris.' She said, '*Paris? Why?*' as if I'd told her Timbuctoo. I said, 'The strip cartoon; there's a paper there that's interested. Anstruther thinks it would help things if I went.' She said, 'Couldn't John go?' and I said, 'Oh, *you* know John,' wishing I hadn't brought him into it, because I'd have to talk to him, now.

She asked, 'How long for?' I said, 'Just the week-end,' and she looked at me, can't *I* come? I said, 'Leaving Friday, seeing him on Saturday, and come back probably on Sunday.' She said, 'All right, darling,' miserably, and I went up behind her and put my arms round her waist, I said, 'You don't mind, honey, do you?' and she said in the same tone, 'No, I don't mind.'

I felt sure she'd got wind of something, but I hadn't got it in me to console her; guilt, partially, but I was angry, too, that I should even need to. It was true, I'd been domesticated, I could see it, now; the doctored cat, let out at regular hours and always back on time, because he knew where he was well off.

We hardly spoke before we got to bed, but when we did she told me suddenly, 'I'm sorry.' I said, 'Sorry for what?' She said, 'For being so demanding. I thought, why doesn't he take *me*? It was just selfish.' I said, 'I would have done.' She said, 'I know you would,' and wriggled close against me, wanting reassurance, me to make love to her. I made myself say, 'We can go next month, just you and I. We can go for a week, if you like.' She said, 'Can we, darling?' and she kissed me while I wished she'd leave me alone. She asked, 'Where are you going to stay?' I said, 'I don't know, it isn't settled, I'll be ringing you,' and she kissed me again, then slid her hand down my thigh, touching my cock, finding it soft, saying, 'Oh, *dar*ling'—you don't love me any more—but I managed it, I did make love to her, and while I did, I thought of Audrey.

CHAPTER FIFTEEN

We flew out.

I'd left Jane the car, and all the way to the airport, on that long, dreary ride along the bypass, past the allotments and the garages and the sterilised white factories, past the rows and rows and rows of ugly little houses, I was wondering if she'd be there, half hoping that she wouldn't; though if she wasn't, *then* what?

I went through passport control; no sign of her, and none in the departure lounge, where people sat like cattle at those coffee tables. *I* couldn't sit, I roamed about the lounge while the flights were called in those prissy Kensington voices, wondering should I phone her, feeling anxious, feeling relieved, feeling God knows what, hearing *our* flight called and sweating, then there she was, beautiful, strolling in calm as could be, wearing a dark-green suit and a tiny green hat.

I rushed to her and said, 'Christ, I thought you weren't coming,' and she smiled and said, 'Of course I was coming.' Then I saw her boarding card, pink, I said, 'First class.' She said, 'Why? Aren't you?' I said, 'No,' pissed off again. She said, 'Never mind, we'll work it out. They may allow me to go slumming.'

So at the plane, the damn great silver jet, she went up one stairway while I waited with the peasants at the other, and watching her climb, so graceful and so certain, I felt that she was climbing away from me, unattainable, I'd never reach her. When she vanished inside the plane, it was as if she'd gone for ever. I wanted to turn back, like the time I'd flown off to Mallorca, and again it was the crowd that stopped me, just the inertia, being caught up with it, a moving staircase, so you just went on among them, up the steps, smiling at the stewardess, into the plane, where they had music playing; Jesus, music everywhere.

It was almost empty, thank Heavens, and I went right up to the front, the end of tourist class, with a spare seat beside me, waiting for her. I'd been looking forward to the take-off, her beside me, to a feeling we'd escaped, we were committed, but now when it came, it did nothing to me. Five minutes, and she hadn't come; ten, twenty with those stupid, damned announcements, the stewardess showing off her lifejacket as if it was a Dior gown. Then there she was, smiling down at me from the doorway, 'Hallo!'

I said, 'Oh, nice of you to come.' She said, 'Yes, isn't it?' and sat down beside me. She was wearing a new perfume, something stronger, almost pungent; I breathed it, then I ran my finger down her cheek, and she turned her head and bit it.

She'd booked us at the Crillon, that toilet-water smell again, better than ever with her because she looked right, she took it all for granted, it was *her*. And Paris was her, as well; the elegance, the beauty, and yet somehow cold, holding something back, something you'd always want but never get.

I went to the window and looked out at that perfect square, then back into the room, at Audrey, standing in the middle of this great big bedroom, perfect, and I wanted to make love to her right then. I came across the floor to her and she looked at me, amused again, that bloody smile. I put my arms round her and kissed her, but she turned her head so I only kissed her cheek, she said, 'Not now.' I said, 'Yes, now, now; why *not* now?' and she shook her head, still smiling. She said, 'We're in Paris,

181

where's your sense of *comme il faut*?' I said, 'I never had one.'

Oh, yes, we were in Paris, *her* Paris, not my lousy tourist's Paris. We were at Les Deux Magots and in the Louvre and on the Île de St Louis and down the Seine along the book barrows and in the little restaurants that she knew — that cost a fortune — and the galleries that she knew and the boutiques; '*Mais quel plaisir, madame!*' And I wished it had been somewhere else, a place that wasn't so much hers, even though the sun still shone and the river looked beautiful and we walked through gardens where the leaves were full on the trees.

The nights were great, though, the nights were wonderful, the nights made up for almost everything, though she still made me feel like she did before; like a stallion, there for service, something to use in bed and laugh at outside. She still had this trick of making me feel stupid, naked; by looking at me, laughing at me, as if even my success was a joke, something I'd thought up to make her laugh.

I wanted to be alone with her all day; *she* wanted to see her friends, and we met them at cafés, in restaurants, little galleries; at a couple of parties where I felt a yokel with my lousy French, and watched them all buzzing round her; painters and writers and that snotty film director again, pretending that he'd never met me.

Yet whatever happened I felt *alive*, and I realised that I hadn't been alive, I'd turned into a vegetable, not happy, not unhappy, just accepting, and that Jane had wanted this, she'd planned for it. It was marvellous, now, to get such quick responses, to make a joke and have it laughed at, not fall flat; to have allusions picked up *zap*, like that, instead of bouncing off a beautiful, blank wall.

I rang Jane that first evening, while Audrey was in the bath. She said, 'How *are* you?' in that exaggerated way, as if I was in China, not in Paris, as if I'd been away a year.

I said, 'All right. I'm at the Crillon, but I'm moving out. It's too expensive.' I didn't want her ringing me. She said, 'I do miss you, darling. Do you realise it's the first time you've been away since we got married?' I said, 'Is it?' then I said, 'I miss you, too.'

Next door, there was a splashing from the bathroom, and I hoped to God she hadn't heard it; any minute, Audrey would be coming out. I said, 'Darling, I'll have to go, I've got to meet this editor, I'll ring you, darling.' She said, 'When?' all anxious, and I said, 'Tomorrow, some time tomorrow,' and blew two quick kisses into the phone and put it down, just as the bathroom door opened.

Audrey came in and asked, 'Was that Jane?' indifferent. She had the bath towel round her; I went over to her and I pulled it off, she let me, smiling, then I bent to kiss her nipple, running my hand over her pubic hair. She didn't move, she said, 'Remember; *comme il faut.*'

I knelt down with my arms around her legs and started kissing her. She said, 'Geoff!' in the same tone, but I didn't stop, and she was quiet, then she sighed, her whole body went stiff and taut, and I pulled her down on the floor beside me.

CHAPTER SIXTEEN

On Sunday night, in bed, she said, 'Let's go to Nice,' and I lay there without answering, stunned. There was only one answer, no, but before I made it, at least I could live with the idea. She asked me, 'Can't you apply for an extension?' She said, 'Try,' and put her lips round my cock, and there was nothing in the world but her and me, us making love.

Next morning, it jolted me awake, just as I'd surfaced and was sinking back again to doze and come up slowly; just a shock at first, a feeling things were wrong, no name to it, and then a word, Nice; oh, Jesus, making it real, something I had to face.

I looked at Audrey there beside me, still asleep, and thought it wasn't real yet, not until she woke. Like most women asleep she looked softer and younger, gentler without a mask of make-up. Her face was turned away from me with her lips parted, almost smiling; one arm stretched upwards, though, across the pillow, as if even in sleep she couldn't quite relax, she was still reaching, struggling. Jesus, how I loved her.

I bent and put her nipple in my mouth and she stirred, she said, 'Insatiable!' then turned, and we made love. Making love, I knew the answer; it was yes, I'd go.

In a way it was surrealist, a kind of parody; we'd been *there* and *there*; that was the hotel where we'd stayed, that was the café where we went in the evenings; that was the place I took Jane dancing; it was like being followed by a ghost. She hadn't believed me, of course; who would? 'He's asked me to join him on his yacht.' What could I tell her? But even with this on my mind, even with the ghosts, it was wonderful; perhaps the ghosts made it so, because soon they'd be real and *these* would be ghosts, so that every hour counted, every minute was alive.

And I thought how ironical it was, how Audrey and I had never been like this, not even when we first lived together, those few weeks at Littlehampton, and now, when things were perfect — the ghosts.

Audrey said, 'I like you better now you're married.' I said, 'Even though I'm fat and domesticated?'

We were lying on a little beach, the only people there; an inlet, just outside Menton. Every day we took the car we'd hired and drove out looking for beaches, beaches that had sand and weren't overrun with people. Audrey wasn't like Jane, she loved the sun, frying herself in sun oil, browner every day, swimming; she was quite a good swimmer, better than me.

She said, 'Yes, you're less demanding. You don't sulk, now.' I said, '*You're* better, too.' She said, 'Because of you.'

The sea was a marvellous, solid blue, dappled with pools of green, shimmering in the sunlight. I tried to be clever, I said, 'Look, the sea's a Renoir,' and she looked and she said, 'No, not a Renoir, a Dufy.' She was wearing sunglasses, the silver kind where you couldn't see her eyes, only yourself looking back at you; it was like her. I said, 'I wish we could go on like this.' She said, 'Come to Corsica, then.' I said, 'Oh, yes. Come to Nice, come to Corsica. And after that to Tangier and Mexico and God knows where.' She laughed and said, 'Why not? Wouldn't you like to?' I said, 'You know I would,' and kissed her shoulder. She said, 'Well, then, come. Get another extension.' I said, 'It would have to be a permanent extension.'

And lying in the sun I knew I would come, like I had before; that I *would* find a way, I had to, however much it cost me, however much I risked, even if it *was* a permanent extension; that if I didn't come, I'd regret it as long as I lived. And at the end of it was something else, just sensed, not even admitted, that if I did come, if I stayed with her, perhaps I'd keep her. Not marry her, necessarily; that might be the way to lose her, but just keep her, have her with me always, have days like these, be *alive*.

I said, 'When would we go to Corsica?' She said, 'Oh, when we get tired of Nice.' And I lay and thought again, this time about John, about the cartoon, it needn't stop me. We were a week ahead, we could easily do it by post, I could phone him. He'd be panicking now, I knew that, and I'd have to get through to him soon or he'd be round with Jane, asking about me, and things would come out, the things he knew; not that I was with Audrey but that I wasn't with the publisher; and I knew him, he might guess about Audrey.

I hardly dared to think about Jane, except that if she'd seen through me, what the hell? In for a penny, in for a pound. I'd been meaning to send her a long letter, telling her phoney things about the yacht, telling her I loved her — I supposed I did, it was so remote — but I couldn't write it, all I'd managed was a postcard: 'Miss you, darling, love, Geoff.'

That night, I told Audrey, 'I'll come with you.' She said, 'What will you tell her?' as if it quite intrigued her. I said, 'God knows.'

It was two days later that we drove to Cannes. I said, 'Cannes? Why? Why don't we look for another beach?' She said, 'No, Cannes. Some people I know might be there.'

So we went and we sat on a commercialised beach in striped deckchairs under a striped umbrella, watching the little dollies and the playboys bouncing and strutting by as brown as cocoa, and the water-skiers skimming behind the motor boats; it was the suntan-lotion world, the toilet-water world moved outdoors, and I didn't belong to it yet, I probably never would. You had to be very young and slim, or spend your time seeing that you *looked* young and slim—and rich, or know someone rich; and I was too fat, not young enough, not rich enough.

We'd been there two or three hours, with Audrey graciously receiving—of course, they all knew her—when she looked out to sea and said, 'I think that's Giorgio.' I said, 'Where?' and she said, 'Water ski-ing. In the white trunks. Don't you think he's graceful?' I said, 'Charming,' and she said, 'Don't be competitive, watch him.'

I said, 'Who is he, anyway?' and she said in a closed, curt voice, 'A Roman,' as if that explained everything, why he was here, why he was brown, why he could water-ski so well.

We were silent, then, because I couldn't speak, I'd nothing to say. I was thinking, she fancies him, he's made love to her; worst of all, thinking, that's probably why she wanted to come; waiting for the moment when the boat came in, when she'd call him over. Until it came, I was here in no-man's-land, left hanging, and I closed my eyes in the sun, hearing the motor boats roar and the French voices playing on the air; the suntan-oil world where I didn't belong; waiting.

I don't know how long it was before I heard her say, '*Mais Giorgio, c'est vraiment toi?*' in a tone I recognised, languid and teasing, and a man's voice, deep, say, '*Oui, ma chère, en effet, c'est moi.*' Then her fingers on my arm and her saying, 'Wake up, Geoff! *Ça c'est mon ami, Geoff Barnes.*' The voice said, '*Enchanté,*' that phoney, bloody word, and I opened my eyes to see him standing above me, a bad way to meet, older than I'd expected, thirty-eightish, black hair cut American style and a bit grizzled, not a fold of stomach, lean legs like a racing cyclist. *I* said, '*Enchanté,*' and put up my hand; he took it in one of those show-off pincer grips, looking at me sort of quizzically; another bastard I amused. His eyes were very dark and knowing; Continental charmer; oh, Christ, I *saw* it.

He said, '*Alors, vous êtes anglais?*' I said, 'Yes,' not *oui*, he could sort that out, and Audrey said, 'Giorgio doesn't talk English, we'll all have to speak French.' *My* French.

He sank down — gracefully — in front of us, as if it was something he'd been practising; or *had* to practise, at his age. Looking at his left hand, I saw he was wearing a gold wedding ring, which somehow made me feel a bit better.

They talked about places they'd both been to and people they both knew who were making the international scene. He was quite polite to me, turning to me every now and then with a great production of courtesy; didn't I think so? did I know them? had I been there? No, of course. No, no, no. Till he asked Audrey did she still water-ski? She said yes, when she was asked, the little flirt, and he said then could he ask her? and she said very well, she would. He gave me his courteous look again, with my permission? Oh, yes, yes, by all means. Perhaps *I* water-skied? No I didn't, actually. Then perhaps I'd join him in the boat. No, thanks, not now. But I *should* learn, really; perhaps he could teach me? Very kind. Well, then ...

Helping her to her feet. Goodbye, Geoff. Exit with him, laughing. I watched them go across the sands, down to the speedboat, still laughing, so easy together, and I watched their bodies sway together, not quite touching, as if they were magnetised, and it was obvious; they'd been lovers.

She sat down and he helped her fit the skis on, climbed into the boat, Audrey took the ropes, and they were off. She looked so great it hurt me; perfectly balanced, brown and slim, hair blowing out in the wind; like something out of reach, quite strange to me, in another dimension, doing something I couldn't do. He was steering one handed, turning round to talk to her; I could imagine them still laughing together, there was nothing that shut you out like laughter. And I wanted to go, get in the car and drive away, knowing now it wouldn't work, it never could; feeling the way she used to make me feel and sooner or later always would.

But then, what would I be going back to? To an empty flat? To Jane, in floods of bloody tears; why had I, how could I? I'd spoken to John and he'd been sullen; I'd asked him how Jane was, and he'd said, '*All* right.' I'd said, 'You haven't told her?' and he'd said, 'No, I *haven't*.' Then he'd said, 'You're with Audrey, aren't you?' — peevish — and I'd told him, 'Let's just say I'm in the South of France.'

So I didn't leave the beach, I felt too demoralised, any decision seemed the wrong one, and I stayed to see what happened, maybe I was wrong, though I knew damn well I wasn't.

I looked for Audrey and the boat, and now I could barely see them, they were so far out to sea; and another thought struck me, that they weren't coming back, which was ridiculous when she'd left her shoes, her sunglasses, her towel, her handbag. I kept on watching them, and now the boat was moving in a curve, back towards the beach, but not to our beach, to some other, farther down the coast. I followed it, followed it, until it turned a head-land and went out of sight, and I was hit by the worst thought yet, he's taking her off to screw her. I looked at my watch; it was one o'clock, people were leaving the beach, others were opening bottles and packets of food. I felt this black rage welling up in me and tried to fight it: if I didn't see them in ten minutes, a quarter-of-an-hour. And ten minutes passed, fifteen, half-an-hour.

By the time I saw the boat again, it was half past two, and she wasn't skiing, now; they were sitting together in the boat. I couldn't bear it, and I couldn't face meeting them. I got up, took my things, left hers, and walked off the beach, to the car. Inside, it was like a furnace, the hot leather seats stuck to the flesh of my legs; I opened the window, but there was barely a breeze. I might have driven off, but I hadn't come here for that, only to get away from them, from her with him. I sat there pouring sweat, without a glimmer of hope, and at last I heard her voice, 'What are *you* doing?'

I didn't look around, I was afraid he was with her, then, when I didn't hear him, when she asked me again, 'What are you *doing*?' I did turn, and she was alone, looking very calm, but surprised—she always did that well—she said, 'Why on earth did you leave the beach to sit here? You left all my things.'

I said, '*You* know.' She said, 'I've no idea.' I just said, 'I want to go back to Nice,' expecting her to disagree, but she said in a humouring voice, 'All right,' and got in the car, just a light beach wrap over her swimsuit. Her leg touched mine, and I thought, it's been touching his. I reached on to the back seat, where I'd slung my shirt, and put it on, then I started the car.

So we drove back without a word, side by side, a thousand miles apart. I knew her too damn well to think there'd be a gesture, an apology, a line you could hang on to; all she said in the end was, 'Why are you being so infantile?' I said, 'Why do you think?' She said, 'You're jealous of Giorgio.' I said, 'He made love to you, didn't he?' She said, 'Don't be so damned silly.' I said, 'You know bloody well he did,' and she said, 'You're really getting paranoid.' I looked at her face; closed, closed. When she spoke again, she said, 'There's no object in our going on, if this is how you behave.' I said, 'How *I* behave!' and then shut up, not trusting myself to speak, till we were back in the hotel, up in our room, when I said to her, 'You did, didn't you?' and she looked right back at me and said, 'You're still impossibly suburban.'

I said, 'Okay.' I lugged my case out of the wardrobe and began to pack it. She said, 'You're like a child,' but I didn't answer, I was trying to shut myself off from everything but this, the packing, the going; taking it moment by moment, changing my clothes, filling the case, locking it, till she walked out into the bathroom, slamming the door, and turned the key. Then I went more slowly, wondering whether there was a plane tonight, knotting my tie in the mirror, remembering that I had to pay the bill.

I could hear her moving about in the bathroom. I wondered if she thought I was bluffing, and I hoped she wouldn't come out, because I didn't want a scene, recriminations, it had gone too far for that.

Then I was ready. I picked up my case, went out of the door and shut it; that was all it was. No tears, no crescendo, nothing, and in a strange way, this was what made it final. A shiver ran through me, and after that, a sudden feeling of relief. I didn't hurry to the lift, nor when I paid the bill. Outside, I got into the car and drove very steadily to the airport. There was a plane for Paris at nine o'clock.

Up in the air I was in limbo; or rather, purgatory, between two hells, the one I'd left and the one that was waiting for me; an empty hell, probably. And I wondered at myself, thinking that I must be mad, to leave what I'd got, what I was sure of, for what I must have known I'd never have, back into the same old trap, thinking things had changed; that *she* had.

At Paris, I changed planes, and walked around that long, smooth departure floor with its sales counters and those pretty, poised salesgirls, wondering, should I get

Jane a present, realising what a parody that would be. On the London plane I suddenly thought, well there's still the camel, and I laughed out loud; the woman next to me drew away, obviously thinking I was crazy.

I took a taxi all the way from London Airport, and when it reached Cromwell Road, getting nearer and nearer home, my heart was thumping; paying it off, my hands shook, and I could hardly count the coins.

The lights were on; I saw that, from the taxi. Standing on the pavement, I looked up at the windows of the living-room, hoping for a glimpse of her, but there was none, and eventually I walked up the steps, took out my keys, and opened the front door. Outside our own door I stopped, listening; nothing. I opened that door, too, and John's voice called, 'Who's that?'

Next moment he came out of the living-room, nervously; then, seeing me, his expression changed; still cautious, but not frightened. He said, 'Hallo ... ' I said, 'Hallo, John,' then over his shoulder he called, 'Geoff's back, Jane. I think perhaps I'll go.' Then he snatched his coat up from a chair and scuttled through the door.

Jane came out. She looked quite ravaged; dead white, sunken cheeks, dark stains beneath her eyes, so wretched she was beyond crying. And it was I who cried, I couldn't stop it, just the sight of her, her being there, I said, 'Jane, Jane!' and put my arms round her neck, sobbing like a child, and after a while I felt her hand on my head, her voice saying, 'Geoff!' then her arm went round me and she guided me into the living-room, on to the sofa, where we sat together, my head in her lap, her stroking it, saying, 'Geoff, my poor darling; Geoff!'

DATE DUE
